We Are Not Meat

The Dino Files – Book 1

Steve Higgs, Hunter Hemsworth Higgs

Text Copyright © 2024 Hunter Higgs & Steve Higgs

Publisher: Steve Higgs

The right of Hunter Higgs and Steve Higgs to be identified as authors of the Work has been asserted by him in accordance with the Copyright, Designs and Patents Act 1988

All rights reserved.

The book is copyright material and must not be copied, reproduced, transferred, distributed, leased, licensed or publicly performed or used in any way except as specifically permitted in writing by the publishers, as allowed under the terms and conditions under which it was purchased or as strictly permitted by applicable copyright law. Any unauthorised distribution or use of this text may be a direct infringement of the author's and publisher's rights and those responsible may be liable in law accordingly.

'We Are Not Meat' is a work of fiction. Names, characters, businesses, organisations, places, events, and incidents either are the product of the author's imagination or are used fictitiously. Any resemblance to actual persons, living, dead or undead, events or locations is entirely coincidental.

Contents

1. Prologue: The Time Thieves — 1
2. Chapter 1 — 5
3. Chapter 2 — 10
4. Chapter 3 — 14
5. Chapter 4 — 21
6. Chapter 5 — 28
7. Chapter 6 — 33
8. Chapter 7 — 39
9. Chapter 8 — 42
10. Chapter 9 — 47
11. Chapter 10 — 57
12. Chapter 11 — 65
13. Chapter 12 — 76
14. Chapter 13 — 84
15. Chapter 14 — 89

16. Chapter 15 — 95
17. Chapter 16 — 104
18. Chapter 17 — 107
19. Chapter 18 — 120
20. Chapter 19 — 134
21. Chapter 20 — 141
22. Chapter 21 — 146
23. Chapter 22 — 152
24. Chapter 23 — 161
25. Chapter 24 — 165
26. Chapter 25 — 170
27. Chapter 26 — 175
28. Chapter 27 — 181
29. Chapter 28 — 190
30. Chapter 29 — 192
31. Chapter 30 — 197
32. Chapter 31 — 199
33. Chapter 32 — 201
34. Chapter 33 — 203
35. Chapter 34 — 207
36. Chapter 35 — 215

37.	Chapter 36	220
38.	Chapter 37	223
39.	Chapter 38	227
40.	Chapter 39	231
41.	Chapter 40	236
42.	Chapter 41	241
43.	Chapter 42	248
44.	Chapter 43	253
45.	Chapter 44	262
46.	Chapter 45	264
47.	Chapter 46	269
48.	Chapter 47	272
49.	Epilogue	275
50.	Author's Note:	278
51.	Free Books and More	281

Prologue: The Time Thieves

Major Grant Blake inspected his team. He knew each of his soldiers very well and had served with them in war zones during their mutual time in the military and in tough situations since. Each man could be depended on to do their job without supervision, to act according to his orders in any given situation, and he knew they would give their lives to protect him if the need arose.

He would do the same for each of them.

Their mission tonight was a simple one, yet it was set to land the team one of the best pay days ever. They were to infiltrate a company headquarters and steal a piece of technology. Put like that it even sounded simple, but to be ready for tonight had taken months of planning.

They'd needed to identify persons within the firm who they could leverage – why break in when someone inside can be bribed or blackmailed into opening the door? It was necessary to have someone on the firm's payroll because the technology they needed to steal wasn't at the company headquarters.

At least not the one located in this time.

To get what they were being paid to steal, they had to travel back in time. All the way back to the Cretaceous era where a firm called Meat Co. was herding dinosaurs and turning them into food. How much would a person pay for a Diplodocus burger or a Stegosaur steak? Well, the answer to that proved to be quite a lot and the owner of Meat Co. was making a fortune.

Leonard Willis was hailed as a visionary by many. A self-made billionaire, it was his technology, the research and development he paid for that made the breakthrough. His firm was the first to achieve time travel, and they were using it to sell food.

Major Blake had no real opinion on the subject. If idiots wanted to spend huge sums to eat something very few would ever taste, he didn't care. However, there were rival firms who desperately wanted to know how Meat Co. did it and since Leonard Willis seemed disinclined to share his firm's proprietary technology, Major Blake's team had been hired to steal it.

Sergeant Hawk looked across at the boss. Major Blake's hair was going grey around the sides, but he had a full head of it, cut short and combed upward to form an out-of-style flat top the man had been sporting for more than two decades. A thin scar ran down the left side of his face from his forehead to his jaw, bisecting his eyebrow to leave it in two parts. At nearly fifty, many might expect him to be losing a step, to no longer be able to cut it with the younger elite soldiers, but if Major Blake was feeling his age, Sergeant Hawk had never seen evidence.

With a dip of his head, Major Blake indicated that it was time, and Sergeant Hawk rallied the troops.

Major Blake watched his right hand man barking orders. Sergeant Hawk was the biggest man in the team. In fact, he was one of the biggest men Major Blake had ever met. Standing six feet and eight inches tall, he was almost as wide, his muscles developed to proportions that could win bodybuilding competitions. In his late thirties, his hair chose to retreat and vanish more than a decade earlier, not that Major Blake cared what his men looked like, not so long as they could do their jobs and each one of his assembled team had been handpicked by him for their abilities.

They expected the mission to be a quick in and out. An hour at most and they would be on their way back to the very building they were currently preparing to leave. However, they knew well enough to be prepared to encounter problems and were armed to the teeth just in case. Just as they would be for any other op.

They would enter the Meat Co. premises in a delivery truck with two of the men disguised as drivers. Their delivery had been logged in advance, so their truck was expected. It was the middle of the night, so the majority of the firm's staff were at home safely tucked up asleep in their beds and they expected no problems on this side.

Morale was high, the soldiers looking forward to the mission more than they normally would simply because they were going to get to see dinosaurs. That they would also be paid for it served as an added bonus.

Setting off into the night, their confidence could not have been higher.

Chapter 1

"Are you ready, kid?" Hudson called from the kitchen.

Rapscallion's eyes flared wide. He had never been more ready in his entire life. It was still a week shy of his ninth birthday, but his dad had organized a special treat and it had to be today, not on his actual birthday next weekend.

Running to the kitchen door, he hung through it at a crazy angle, beyond excited at what they were about to do. At very nearly nine he was big for his age. He had his mother's blonde hair and blue eyes, in contrast to his father's dark brown hair and brown eyes. His dad was tall at six feet and two inches, and lean like an athlete which showed off the muscle he'd developed during his time in the British Army.

Rapscallion's own muscles were yet to grow, though his father insisted they would get around to it soon enough if he was patient.

"Am I ready?" he gasped. "I couldn't be more ready! I'm so ready I might burst if we don't go soon!"

His father laughed, bending to place one knee on the kitchen tile so his son could come in close for a hug.

As they clung to each other, Hudson whispered, "Then let's get going."

They broke their hug, Rapscallion's dad jumping back to his feet energetically. He snatched a backpack from the kitchen counter, slipping it over his shoulders while patting his pockets to make sure he had everything.

Rapscallion was already halfway to the front door.

"Come on, Dad!" he called back through the house.

Hudson couldn't help the grin spreading across his face. It had been a tough couple of years; Rapscallion's mum died just before his seventh birthday, but they were strong together and Hudson knew his son was a great kid.

That's why he was taking such a risk to give him the best ninth birthday any boy had ever dreamed of. They were going on the trip of a lifetime, going somewhere very few could ever afford: back to the time of the dinosaurs.

Hudson's brother, Rapscallion's uncle, worked at Meat Co., a firm the whole world was talking about. Their boffins invented time travel; Hudson could remember the huge news coverage their announcement caused when they unveiled their technology.

They were the only ones with it, though there were many other firms trying to match what Meat Co. had achieved. The technology was worth a fortune, of course, and the people at Meat Co. were exploiting their market position.

You might think they could go forward into the future where they could discover new inventions and bring them back to our time, but apparently time travel doesn't work like that. You cannot go forward beyond the time when you live. Not even by a day. Going back though, that works just fine.

Meat Co. was travelling sixty-five million years into the past where in the late Cretaceous period they were herding dinosaurs and bringing them back to the present to be served as food. They also ran tours, but only for the mega rich. A single ticket to go back to the past cost a million pounds, and Hudson didn't have the kind of job that was going to pay enough to afford to buy one.

He didn't like that the dinosaurs were being exploited and herded like so many cows, but neither he nor Rapscallion were vegetarians, so in principle, this was no different from eating a steak or a lamb chop.

"Come on, Dad!" Rapscallion's overexcited shout broke Hudson from his daydream and got his feet moving.

In their car, Hudson reminded his son about what they needed to do when they got to the Meat Co. base.

"I know, Dad," Rapscallion replied, doing his best not to sound impatient with his father. This had to be the fifth time they had gone over it today. He chose to shortcut his dad's lecture and recite the plan himself. "We don't have permission to be there. Uncle Ralph is sneaking us in through one of the back doors after hours because this is the only way we can get to the time travel portal. We have to stay quiet, keep out of sight, but also look like we are supposed to be there when we have to traverse through any of the open areas. Uncle Ralph has uniforms and official passes for us and has made arrangements with the people working tonight so as long as we don't run into anyone from management, we shouldn't have any problems. When we arrive at Time Base Alpha in the Cretaceous, Uncle Ralph will lead us to one of the Time Tour Rovers and take us on a two-hour dinosaur safari."

Hudson made an impressed face. His son *had* been listening.

WE ARE NOT MEAT

"We get two hours between the guard rotations to explore the Cretaceous," Rapscallion's voice betrayed how excited he was at the prospect, raising in volume and getting faster, "where we will see hundreds of dinosaurs!"

Hudson laughed again. He seemed to do that a lot around his son.

"That's right, kid. That's right. But ..." he drawled the word, "What do we need to remember when we are observing the dinosaurs?"

Rapscallion tutted to himself; he'd forgotten the most important part.

"We need to keep our eyes peeled for carnivores and pay attention to the Jeep's proximity warning system. That will tell us if anything dangerous is close."

"It should do," said Hudson. "We just need to make sure we don't get too carried away looking at the herbivores and end up as a meal for a Tarbosaurus."

With that thought echoing in their minds, they both fell silent, excited yet aware that what they were proposing to do was far from devoid of risk.

Chapter 2

"This way," Uncle Ralph beckoned.

They were inside the main Meat Co. building. The operation occupied a huge area on the north bank of the Thames estuary to the east of London. The drive had taken almost two hours despite the fact that they could see the plant from the upstairs of their house. They were on the wrong side of the river though and had to go the long way to get there.

Rapscallion imagined it was all one building – while he could see the plant from his house it was too far away to make out the details. It wasn't though and he only got to appreciate the full scale of the operation as they drew closer to it.

The buildings themselves were enormous. Massive. Gargantuan even. Rapscallion wasn't sure any of those words were sufficient to do justice to just how big the place was. It wasn't just big. It was BIG.

And they were inside it and on their way to the time travel portal.

Rapscallion couldn't help but look around, his eyes wide with wonder. Around his neck hung the pass Uncle Ralph gave him. He held onto it with his right hand, absentmindedly gripping it as if to reassure himself this was really happening.

Uncle Ralph had also given them uniforms to wear. They were the same style as his, a dark grey, light grey, and almost purple mix of small block colours like a soldier would wear. Uncle Ralph also had a gun, a small automatic pistol in a holster on his right hip.

Rapscallion had never touched a gun. He'd rarely even seen one except when they went to the airport that one time and the police there were carrying Heckler and Koch machine guns. He wouldn't have known what they were, but his father knew all about such things. His dad didn't talk about that part of his life much, but Rapscallion had seen the photographs and knew his dad served with the Special Air Service, the military's most elite fighting force.

"Heeeeeere we are!" announced Uncle Ralph, his voice like that of a game show host revealing the grand prize.

Rapscallion had been looking to his right, not ahead, and had to swing his eyes around to see what had gotten Uncle Ralph so excited.

He didn't need to be told what it was he was seeing though. The object to his front required no explanation. Granted, it said 'Time Travel Portal' in six-foot-high letters right above it, but Rapscallion would have been able to guess what it was without the label.

The portal looked like a giant TV screen. It was flat and black and measured about forty feet across by twenty feet high. It sat perhaps five feet off the floor with a short, gentle ramp leading up to it.

The black surface trapped between the frame had a strange appearance, like it was actually liquid somehow suspended vertically. Ink, Rapscallion decided, it looked like ink.

Uncle Ralph hadn't broken his stride, but turned to walk backward now, his arms extended on either side and a wide grin on his face.

"This is the time travel portal," he announced needlessly, "but you could probably figure that out for yourselves."

Hudson reached forward with his right arm, grabbing his brother's hand to give it a firm shake.

WE ARE NOT MEAT

"This is amazing, Ralph. You really came through for us."

"Hey, what are brothers for?"

Rapscallion's dad didn't answer. Not because he had nothing to say, but because it had just become clear something was wrong.

Chapter 3

"What are you doing here, Ralph?" asked a man coming their way. He'd just exited a door at the bottom of a tower that looked down onto the time travel portal floor.

Rapscallion hadn't noticed the tower until the man spoke, but looking at it now, he could see it was the control room for the portal itself.

The man's steps were hurried, his eyes haunted like there was something deeply amiss and it was causing him to worry.

Uncle Ralph looked equally concerned and Rapscallion felt his heart sink. He knew Uncle Ralph was bending the rules just to let them into the plant. Arranging for them to use the time travel portal was probably enough to get him fired if anyone found out, but he'd insisted repeatedly that it wouldn't be a problem.

Now it looked as if that wasn't the case. Were they about to get kicked out of the building? Or would the man hurrying their way call the cops?

Uncle Ralph frowned. "What's up, John? Is there a problem?"

John quickened his steps again, closing the final yards, the panic never leaving his eyes.

Rapscallion felt his father's hand grip his shoulder, keeping him still. He looked up to meet his dad's eyes and got to see him put a finger to his lips – it was time to stay quiet.

"What are you doing here?" the man called John repeated his question.

Ralph used an arm to steer John to one side, taking him away from Rapscallion and his dad but not so far that they couldn't hear what was being said.

"We talked about this earlier, John," Uncle Ralph replied, his tone hard and bordering on angry. "I've got my brother and his kid here, remember? They are going through for a couple of hours, that's all."

"That's tonight?" John sounded like he had his dates mixed up.

"Yes, John," Uncle Ralph shook his head. "Look they are here. They've done the hard part. I'll take them through, they can poke around and see the dinosaurs and be back before anyone knows. You're the one who told me no one would notice an extra unplanned portal opening because they are doing so much testing at the moment."

Unable to stay quiet, Rapscallion whispered, "Are we going to get to travel, Dad?"

Hudson had been watching his brother and listening to his conversation with John, the man from the control tower. It wasn't going well. John was clearly nervous about something. Was he expecting his supervisor to show up? Was that it? Had Ralph miscalculated and they were all about to get into trouble.

Crouching slightly so he could return his son's whisper, Hudson said, "I don't know, Rap. Let's just give it a minute and see. If not tonight, then I'm sure Uncle Ralph will be able to reorganize it for another time."

"But I'm ready now," Rapscallion whined, desperate to see the dinosaurs.

His uncle had moved closer to John, getting his mouth up against the man's ear so his words could no longer be heard. Rapscallion had no idea what Uncle Ralph said but it made the other man's eyes go wide.

Stepping back so he could look John in the eyes, Uncle Ralph said, "So we are in agreement?"

John did not look happy. "It's not like you're giving me any choice, Ralph. Just be back on time, okay? You're not the only 'guests' traveling tonight."

Uncle Ralph spun around to face his brother and Rapscallion, clapping his hands together and beaming a big smile.

"Everyone ready then? Let's time travel!"

Rapscallion punched the air and whooped, "Yeah! Let's go see some dinosaurs."

John hurried away to the tower without once looking back in their direction.

Hudson watched him go, and as his brother led them to the portal, he quietly asked, "Everything okay?"

"Sure, sure, absolutely," Ralph lied.

Hudson knew he was lying because they were brothers, and he knew when his brother wasn't telling the truth.

Withering under Hudson's accusing gaze, Ralph huffed out a breath.

"Okay, fine. John managed to double book tonight. I don't know how, but he said he'd got some other friends that already went through. He's a little worried that sending us through as well will ... well, it will be too many unexpected people in the same place."

Hudson gripped his brother's arm to show he was serious. "Look, we don't have to do this tonight."

"But Rapscallion is so excited to go."

"We can go another time," Hudson argued.

Ralph stopped walking. "Look, it's fine, okay? I leaned on John a little because he's been stealing meat supplies and selling them under the counter to restaurants in London. He's making a killing and I suggested he might not want to give me a reason to point out the brand-new car he's driving that he ought not to be able to afford on his wages."

Hudson shook his head – his brother was a rogue, but it seemed as though there was nothing much to worry about and Ralph was coming through the portal with them anyway. He was most likely worrying about nothing.

They reached the start of the ramp leading up to the portal. Now they were so close, Rapscallion truly got a sense of how big it was. It needed to be, he understood, because they drove trucks through it. Meat Co. had built a complete base on the other side, and all the materials required had to go through the portal. It was a big operation.

While the science behind time travel was a mystery Rapscallion couldn't hope to understand, he knew that you could only travel to the exact same location you were already in. The time portal couldn't take you from present day London to ancient Greece, it could only open at the same place in London.

Of course, they were travelling so far back in time, the location couldn't be called London. It was just a patch of rock that would one day become the nation's capital. Right now they were next to the river Thames, but Uncle Ralph said there was no river where they were going. The landmasses, the plates upon which they sat, were constantly moving and they would change unrecognisably over the course of the next sixty-five million years.

John's voice came over Uncle Ralph's radio, "Portal is now active, Ralph. If you are going, now is the time."

The message would have come over the control tower's personal address system for normal operations, but they were sneaking through, and it had to be kept quiet.

"Ready?" Uncle Ralph grinned.

Rapscallion grabbed his father's hand. He was too big to be holding hands with his dad, but this was different. They were about to time travel and though excited beyond belief, Rapscallion was also utterly terrified.

"How many times have you done this?" he asked his uncle.

Uncle Ralph stepped right up to the shimmering wall of black liquid suspended in the air. Holding his right hand half an inch from the surface, he twisted his upper half around to look back at his nephew.

"Oh, only about a thousand times."

With that, he made a big show of gasping in a lungful of air to hold his breath, grabbed Rapscallion's other hand, and walked into the black liquid taking his nephew with him.

Chapter 4

Rapscallion felt a tugging sensation in his stomach, then what can only be described as his body elongating. Not from his toes to his head, but from his front to his back. He felt a mile thick.

It only lasted for a half second, but the sensation was going to stay with him forever.

Stepping into the black liquid, his vision had gone, much as it might if diving into a pool of ink. Then it was back just as quickly, and he was looking out at a completely different scene.

For a start there were dinosaurs.

Hundreds of them.

To his left was a huge pen filled with hadrosaurs making gentle bleating/mooing noises. Rapscallion listened, trying to work out whether they sounded more like a cow than a sheep.

Whichever it was, they sounded like no animal he'd ever heard before.

Beyond them, another pen reached to the ceiling at least thirty feet above their heads. There were sauropods in it, giant beasts with long necks and tails that seemed to stretch on forever.

Rapscallion started forward, his legs moving of their own accord only to be stopped when a hand snagged hold of his top.

"Whoa there, kiddo," whispered his dad. "Remember we are not supposed to be here."

"But we are wearing Meat Co. uniforms," Rapscallion hissed back.

"Uh-huh. But how many eight-year-old employees do you think they have?"

"I'm almost nine."

Hudson gave his son a disapproving look. "Same difference, buddy. The uniform is to help us blend in at a distance. We don't want anyone to be able to spot that you are not just a really short adult."

"But, Dad, look at the sauropods," Rapscallion pleaded. "Just look at how big they are! We can go right over there and touch them through the cages. Are they..." He turned to look at Uncle Ralph, "are they Diplodocus?"

Uncle Ralph shot his nephew a lopsided grin. "You have a good eye, my man. They are Diplodocus. But your dad is right – we can't be hanging around in here. The best thing for us to do is stick with the plan and get you guys outside. It's daytime here so you get a couple of hours to explore close to the base. You'll see plenty of herbivores in their natural environment and that's much better than seeing these ones on their way to the processors."

Rapscallion cringed a little. He knew Meat Co. was slaughtering the dinosaurs to bring them back as food and seeing the harmless giants stuck in cages made him feel a little sick.

"Come on," said Uncle Ralph, heading down the ramp and to the left. "Let's get into a dino rover and be on our way."

Rapscallion looked back at the time portal. The black shimmering liquid looked exactly as it had before, there was no sign of their passage.

He was still looking that way when a shot rang out through the still air.

His father and uncle both froze instantly, the sound of the gunshot's echoes fading away. Rapscallion looked at his father, a quiver of concern easing through his belly. His dad looked worried and that almost never happened.

Hudson was looking at his brother, an obvious question forming on his lips, but Uncle Ralph's equally mystified expression made it clear he couldn't explain why they had all just heard someone fire a gun.

Two seconds ticked by; enough time for Rapscallion's heartrate to spike and begin to settle again. Perhaps it was nothing after all. A misfire or something, not a guard trying to stop a rampaging T-Rex.

However, before he could draw his next breath, the air filled with the unmistakable sound of rapid machine gun fire.

Hudson grabbed hold of Rapscallion's top, running with him faster than the eight-year-old's legs could go. He was aiming for cover, a gap between some big crates. Uncle Ralph was leading, his head down and his sidearm now out, held low and at the ready.

The sight of his uncle's weapon no longer in its holster made Rapscallion gasp. Whatever was happening, it was neither expected nor normal. Uncle Ralph's head and eyes moved constantly, swinging in one direction and the next as he searched for any sign of danger.

"What's going on!" Rapscallion cried, no longer worried whether he would get to see the Cretaceous era and explore, but scared they might be in serious danger. The bullets were still flying, and to Rapscallion's ears it sounded like two sets of people shooting at each other, not someone trying to defend the base against a carnivore.

The trio reached the crates where Hudson threw himself to the floor. Pulling his son with him, they slid the last few feet to get into cover. Rapscallion might have asked why they needed to hide had a volley of bullets not smacked into the crates a few yards above their heads.

"They're shooting at us!" he panicked.

Rapscallion had more he wanted to say; his nerves were on edge, and he'd never been more scared, but his father's hand over his mouth stopped him.

"Shhhh," Hudson urged his son. "They were wild shots, not aimed at us. They missed their intended target, son, but this is a dangerous place to be, and we need to get back home."

Hudson swung his head around to check with his brother.

Uncle Ralph's sidearm, a small calibre automatic pistol, was pointing back out of the gap between the crates, covering the way they had come.

The shooting continued and it was coming closer. They could all hear running footsteps, multiple heavy boots on the concrete floor of the base.

"Ralph," growled Hudson. "What is going on?"

Ralph shot his brother a look that said, *'I've got no clue'*, and replied with, "I don't know. The best thing we can do is get back through the portal, but I need to get to the tower guys to get them to activate it."

"Where's that?" asked Hudson.

Uncle Ralph pointed with his free hand. It was all the way back across the open area in front of the time portal and the boots and gunfire were still coming their way.

"Well, we can't just sit here," shouted Hudson, a determined edge to his voice. Rapscallion knew the tone; it was the one his father used when he'd done something he shouldn't have. His dad meant business and to Rapscallion's mind that meant things were going to get done.

The dinosaurs in their pens were getting noisy, the alien sound of gunfire causing them to panic. The hadrosaurs, enormous beasts capable of running on two legs, were more than restless. They trumpeted their fear, filling the time base with even more noise, and bashed against the sides of the steel cage that held them.

Rapscallion saw when their combined mass tried to move in one direction to get away from the harsh sound of gunfire. The bolts holding the pen to the floor shifted, several wrenching free of the concrete. The entire cage shifted a foot across the floor, the hadrosaurs inside bumping and bashing into each other. The thick steel holding them in place wasn't going to hold forever.

Making a decision, Hudson rose from his crouch behind the stack of crates. Touching his son's shoulder, he said, "Rap, we're going to have to cut this excursion short. Okay?"

Rapscallion nodded his head vigorously. He'd been desperate to come here and beyond excited at the prospect of seeing real dinosaurs in their natural habitat. Right now though, the only thing he wanted was to be tucked up safely in his bed.

Hudson peeked out to get a better view of the platform and the time portal. Ducking back into cover, he said, "Ralph, you get to the tower. Get the portal open, and then let's get out of here."

Uncle Ralph didn't look like he was entirely happy with the plan, but they had to do something, and he nodded silently before stepping out in to the open.

That was when it happened.

Chapter 5

The entire floor of the Meat Co. base rocked, an explosion ripping through the building. Rapscallion lost his footing, coming down to one knee so he wouldn't fall over. He turned toward the sound of the blast which meant he was looking in the right direction when a ball of flame filled the air.

It was on the other side of the building, but he could feel the heat from it. Moments later a rush of air pushed outward by the explosion brought dust and dirt. It tore at their clothing and whipped their hair.

It also proved the last straw for the hadrosaurs who ran at the walls of their pen, battering two panels open where they joined.

Meat Co. workers, who had been trying to calm the dinosaurs, ran for their lives. Not fast enough though for Rapscallion got to watch with horror as three or four were run over in the stampede. One of the guards, sensing that he couldn't get away in time, started firing at the dinosaurs. His shots were wild and panicked, but with so many targets he still struck home.

The hadrosaurs tried to avoid him, bumping and bouncing off each other as they raced to be anywhere else. The guard's tactic might have worked, but shooting a looming hadrosaur dead, he failed to consider where it would land.

Rapscallion looked away but he heard the guard's final terrified squeal before the three-ton dinosaur squashed him flat.

Shouting voices had been coming their way almost since the first shots were fired. Now they were close, and Hudson believed they either got moving now or they risked being caught up in whatever was going on.

"We've got to go!" he bellowed to be heard above the din of noise echoing inside the Meat Co. time base.

Leaving their position of relative cover was scary, but staying put wasn't an option either. Holding his dad's hand, Rapscallion ran as fast as he could. They raced toward the time portal. That was their avenue of escape, but they needed Uncle Ralph to get it open again.

They were halfway across the platform when the distant shouts became infinitely clearer. Hudson turned his head to see men running into the open. He counted a dozen men, each carrying automatic weapons and running just as fast as they could. They were coming right for them.

They wanted to exit through the time portal too!

Right before his eyes, Rapscallion saw some of the armed men turn and fire back the way they had come. They were dressed all in black. It made them look like soldiers, but these were not Meat Co. workers; they were something else.

Uncle Ralph was just over halfway to the tower, but caught in the open with a dozen armed men heading right for him, he abandoned his quest to get to the time portal control tower and ran for cover instead.

Hudson likewise changed strategy. Yanking Rapscallion along in his wake, he ran straight across the front of the time portal platform and into cover on the other side.

"Dad! What are we doing?" Rapscallion yelled, barely able to hear his own voice over the gunfire, stampeding dinosaurs, shouting, and a claxon that had just started in reaction to the fire now spreading as a result of the explosion.

Hudson held his son close, using his body to shield him. Crouching to get his mouth close to Rapscallion's ear, he shouted, "Avoiding danger, kid! We're going to let these guys get past us. Whoever they are, I reckon they are the cause of all the trouble. We let them get through the time portal, and once they are gone we can try to get home ourselves."

"Where's Uncle Ralph!" Rapscallion might have cried if it had occurred to him to do so. He was scared enough, but he also recognized there was nothing to be gained by shedding tears. He needed a clear head and to be ready to move when his father told him to go.

Hudson checked, but he couldn't see his brother. He took that to be good news. If Ralph wasn't lying on the concrete, he had made it into cover and was just out of sight for now.

The armed gunmen in their black uniforms were running straight for the portal. They had a trolley with them, on which they were wheeling something too heavy to carry. Two of the men were pushing it from the sides with a third steering from the back.

From their vantage point tucked between machinery to one side of the time portal, Rapscallion and Hudson watched. The men with the trolley shoved it over the lip of the ramp and up onto the platform.

They ran in a tight formation, the men not involved in moving the trolley surrounding it to give cover.

In seconds they would reach the wall of shimmering black liquid, and if it was activated, they would vanish through it, leaving the way clear for others to escape.

Rapscallion couldn't take his eyes off them. They were all big men; as big as his dad at least and not just tall, they were muscular too.

Now that they were closer, his curiosity made him lean out to get a better look. They were being led by a man with grey hair. He looked to be ten or more years older than everyone else. Older than Rapscallion's dad even, and he was nearly forty! Like the rest of the soldiers in black, the leader's hair was cut short though it was styled upwards and trimmed to be flat on top.

As if he could somehow feel Rapscallion's gaze, the man turned to look his way.

Rapscallion met the blue-eyed gaze of the group leader and held it for a count of two. Unable to look away, Rapscallion was still staring right at him when the leader smiled and raised his gun.

He was going to shoot them!

Chapter 6

Rapscallion's heart simply stopped beating.

Hudson saw the threat too and threw himself backwards to get further into the cavity in which they were hiding. Pushing Rapscallion behind his own body, he tensed, expected bullets to start hitting the spot they had just vacated, though thankfully none came.

Oh, there was plenty of gunfire still, but when he dared to peek out, he saw the armed men firing back at the Meat Co. guards. The guards were outnumbered- it was only a handful of them, and they were outmatched, but they were doing their best.

Hudson just wanted the time portal to open so the men in black could escape. That would effectively end the fight and remove the immediate danger, but the guards were firing right at the men standing in front of the time portal structure, so it was probably inevitable they would hit it.

Sparks flew and another alarm wailed into life as if the world needed any more noise in it.

The wall of black liquid stopped shimmering, stuttered once, twice, and vanished completely to reveal what lay behind it – more of the Meat Co. building.

The time portal was broken!

The men in black saw it too, their answer to return even heavier fire as they surged back across the time portal platform. Mercifully, they went away from Hudson and Rapscallion, racing to find cover.

They continued shooting at the guards until the last man zipped through a gap between machines and the terrifying group disappeared from sight.

The shooting stopped abruptly, but it didn't make much difference to the overall noise inside the Meat Co. base. Dinosaurs were still trumpeting their terror. It was impossible to see how many had escaped their pens, but Rapscallion could hear the clanging sound of metal reverberating as more tried to break free. The diplodocuses were nowhere in sight, though now that he was looking Rapscallion saw a tall head poking up through the smoke gathering near the roof.

The fire, whether started by the explosion or not, was raging, orange flames flickering to the ceiling.

Still peering out from their hiding space, Rapscallion cried out in fright when a figure appeared in front of his face without warning.

"Guys!" Uncle Ralph breathed a sigh of relief. "Are you both okay?" He was checking them for bullet wounds.

"We're fine!" Hudson shouted back. "We can't stay here though. Can the time portal be fixed?" He doubted that would be the case and knew his brother wouldn't know the answer, but it had to be asked.

Uncle Ralph shook his head. "No idea, but the building is on fire! We have to get you guys out of it right now." To accentuate his point, a curl of smoke drifted by, tickling their throats unpleasantly.

Being a man of action, Hudson didn't waste time on words. He started moving, leaving their hiding place and asking, "Where?"

"I'll get you to one of the rovers." Uncle Ralph led them at a jog. "You'll be stuck here until the tech guys can get the portal working again."

"How long will that be?" Rapscallion asked, worried he wasn't going to like the answer.

Uncle Ralph pulled a face like he was sucking on a lemon. "No way to guess, Rap, sorry. Might be hours. Might be days. They might need parts they haven't got here and if that's the case they will have to wait until they get sent through from the present. The good news is that the portal can be opened from the other side still."

Confused, Hudson asked, "How does that work?"

Uncle Ralph just shrugged his shoulders. "Beats me. It's super clever science fiction stuff if you ask me. The whole time travel thing is."

Rapscallion, pleased to know more than the adults for once, volunteered what he knew.

"It's all to do with temporal displacement," he recited some of the words he could recall from an article he'd watched on YouTube. Not certain he was explaining it right, he pressed on anyway. "They can only travel backwards in time, right."

"That's how I understand it," Uncle Ralph remarked, continuing to lead them through the increasingly smoke-filled passageways between machinery and equipment.

"So they can get here, but once they step through, they need someone in the present to open the portal again so they can get back. Having a portal here allows them to connect to the portal in our time era and open it for themselves from this end."

Hudson was impressed by his son's knowledge of the subject but had a question, "Why don't they just keep it open the whole time?"

"Ah," Uncle Ralph interrupted. He knew the answer to that particular question. "Generating the time portal requires an enormous amount of energy. They have a nuclear reactor here just to power the device when they do want to open it."

Hudson gritted his teeth. They were stuck here until someone from the other side opened the portal. That might happen in five seconds or five hours and the fire was still spreading, the smoke getting thicker. They needed to vacate the building until it was safe to come back inside.

When they did that, he was certain they were going to get caught; the one thing he prayed wouldn't happen. It would cost Ralph his job for sure and might mean criminal charges. It had seemed worth the risk so his son could see the dinosaurs he was so mad about. Now it felt like his decision to break the rules was foolish and likely to end in disaster.

Regardless, there was nothing he could do about it, so he didn't waste his breath getting upset or questioning who to blame.

However, he did want to know one thing.

"Who were those guys in black? And why was Grant Blake leading them?"

Chapter 7

Uncle Ralph's reply came as a question. "Who is Grant Blake?"

"Former major in the SAS. He was there at the same time as me. He wasn't exactly popular and got kicked out of the army when he was found guilty of war crimes in Afghanistan. He's not a nice guy. I take it the team of guys in black were here to steal whatever was on that trolley?"

They were weaving through the building still, Uncle Ralph leading them to the dino rovers they would use to escape, but it felt like they had gone half a mile already, the place was so vast. Unavoidably, with the wailing alarm, the trumpeting, panicked dinosaurs, and the smoke, they didn't spot the squad of guards coming their way until it was too late.

Whether Uncle Ralph knew who Major Blake's team were or what might have been on the trolley had to wait because his boss was among the guards, and he'd spotted them.

"Oh, cripes. That's Captain Cutter," Uncle Ralph cursed.

"Gilbert!" a man who was clearly in charge barked at Uncle Ralph using his last name. "What are you doing here and who are these people?"

Uncle Ralph promised there would be no problem sneaking them in so they could go back in time to see the dinosaurs and that was proving to be about as far from the truth as possible. It wasn't his fault, but that didn't change that they were now caught in the act of trespass and were going to find themselves in deep trouble.

"Captain Cutter," Uncle Ralph choked out the name of his boss. "I um ..."

Captain Cutter looked around Uncle Ralph, staring straight at Rapscallion and his dad. He narrowed his eyes, scrutinizing their faces.

"Let me guess. You snuck some family through the portal for a little joyride." Captain Cutter aimed his eyes at Uncle Ralph again who withered a little under his boss's gaze. "We'll deal with this later. Right now I need you and everyone else still alive to help fight the fire and save this base. Come with me."

Captain Cutter turned to find the men he was with all watching.

"What are you idiots doing! Can't you hear the alarm? That's the temperature warning on the reactor coolant system! Get to the fire and help whoever is there to get it under control! Don't wait for me!" He shouted at their backs as they ran down the passageway and out of sight.

Uncle Ralph was yet to move. "Sir, what about my brother and his kid?"

"Do I look like I care?" snapped the captain. "You brought them here. They are your baggage, and I don't have time to be babysitting civilians. Put them somewhere safe and get to the fire. If we don't get it under control soon we might lose the whole building. It's right next to the nuclear reactor."

Rapscallion saw his dad and uncle exchange a look.

"The nuclear reactor?" Hudson repeated.

Chapter 8

Leonard Willis was not the sort of person who liked to hear bad news. He was known for firing people who brought him bad news.

A self-made billionaire, he believed a person delivering bad news was admitting they were unable to resolve the situation that led to the news being bad. That showed incompetence and he had no need to employ incompetent people.

That was why Timothy Moore, Chief Operating Officer at Time Base UK, the hub of Leonard's entire time travel operation, chose instead to call Leonard's second in command, a fierce woman called Stacey Longbridge.

When Stacey subsequently called Leonard, waking him from a blissful sleep far too many hours before the sun would rise, he vowed immediately to fire Timothy Moore. It didn't even matter what the problem was or whether he had it all under control already. In calling Stacey he showed a lack of backbone and that was enough to warrant his dismissal.

Storming through the doors to the offices high above and overlooking Time Base UK, he growled, "What is it then? What mess have you all created that I must now fix?" He expected it would be something to do with the government. The politicians were all over Leonard and Meat Co. insisting his operation needed legally binding regulations and the control of a government body to ensure nothing they did could endanger anyone. Of course, politicians were all weak and small minded in Leonard's opinion.

Was it his fault there were no rules to govern time travel and what he could use the technology for? Of course not. He'd invested billions into research to make his dreams become a reality. Now he got to reap the benefits of his vision and he refused to let the government step in to limit what he could do.

Sure, some of what he was doing could cause financial instability on a global scale, and he was one hundred percent certain the world would frown on his black-market sales of dinosaur eggs and small species dinosaurs as exotic pets, but it was his technology that made it all possible. How dare they attempt to tell him what he could do with it?

No one responded to his question, the faces around the room all glancing at each other as though begging someone else to start talking. Timothy Moore looked positively pale, but when

Leonard met his eyes, his mouth opened and he prepared to start talking.

"No, not you, Timothy. You're fired. Get out." Leonard nodded to a pair of burly security guards hovering just outside the meeting room's glass door. They stepped in at his non-verbal command, but they didn't have to remove the Chief Operating Officer, he walked silently from the room leaving the remaining staff looking stunned.

"Well!" Leonard barked, not used to being made to wait. Even his most trusted lieutenant, Stacey Longbridge, was looking a little green around the gills at the prospect of having to break the bad news.

However, when he aimed his irate gaze solidly in her direction, she accepted her role and started to explain.

"We are detecting radiation at levels which indicate Time Base Alpha has suffered a major reactor incident."

Leonard had been guessing what bad news they might have for him ever since he'd been woken from his slumber, but an incident with the reactor had never occurred to him.

His eyes widening, he asked, "How sure are you?"

Stacey shook her head. "No one has come back through the portal for four hours, Sir. Routine maintenance crews, security shift swaps, and more than three dozen scientists were due to have returned here in that time. We suspect something catastrophic has befallen Time Base Alpha."

Leonard's head suddenly felt fuzzy. He reached for a chair, his fingers fumbling to grip it properly on his first attempt. Slumping into it, he considered the gravity of the news. This wasn't bad news, this was the worst it could possibly be. His operation was ruined.

"The portal will still open from this side though, right?"

"Yes," Stacey replied cautiously, "but sending anyone back could mean instant death if there is a radiation leak."

"Then give them protective suits!" Leonard roared, losing his cool and shouting loud enough to startle everyone in the room. "I want to know for sure. Then I want to know what we can do about it." He fell silent, just for a few seconds until a new thought occurred to him. "What is the current radiation reading?"

Stacey looked across the room to Edgar McHarry, the firm's chief scientist.

"The reading I took less than half an hour ago was fifty-three millisieverts. That's about three times what you would get during a hospital CT scan and perfectly safe. We are not in any danger here."

Leonard's brow furrowed. "So what's the big deal? That doesn't sound too bad."

Edgar bit his lip before continuing to carefully explain, "That's the reading today, Mr Willis. It will have been falling for sixty-five million years. My calculations indicate the radiation level at Time Base Alpha must have reached a level close to twenty thousand millisieverts. Exposure to a dose that strong, even for a fraction of a second, would kill a person within a week. There is no chance anyone could survive it."

Leonard's jaw dropped. How could it be that bad? What could possibly have happened at Time Base Alpha?

Chapter 9

The answers to all Leonard's questions were still being discussed amid the smoke and drama inside Time Base Alpha.

Captain Cutter had just revealed how close the fire was to the nuclear reactor, but they didn't know what the scientists in the future had already figured out – that the base was beyond saving.

Repeating his question, Hudson was unable to keep the worry from his voice when he asked, "The reactor is in danger?"

"Yes, and it's already displaying multiple warning signs and has started to vent excess pressure into the atmosphere. I believe the explosion was meant to cover the thieves' escape, but it may also have cracked the cooling tubes circulating water around the reactor. If that's the case and we don't get the fire under control ..." He placed his hands together and mimed the building exploding.

Rapscallion didn't know anything about nuclear reactors, but he'd learned about nuclear bombs in school and didn't want to be anywhere nearby if there was going to be an explosion.

He believed they needed to be moving as fast as they could toward an exit, but his dad was still asking questions about Major Blake and his team of heavily armed soldiers.

"The explosion was set off by the team of soldiers? I know their boss. They had something on a trolley and I'm guessing it was valuable."

Captain Cutter reacted instantly. "You know them?" His hand shot down to grab the handgun holstered on his right hip. "Are you part of their group?"

Hudson almost moved to intercept the captain's hand before he could pull his gun, but he'd faced men with guns many times before and could tell Cutter wasn't about to do anything. It was a show of bravado meant to make him look tough and nothing more.

"No," Hudson replied calmly, his hands still by his sides. "I'm not with them and I would have to be fairly stupid to mention knowing their leader if I was. But I want to know if I am right to assume they caused the explosion."

Seeing the lack of threat, Captain Cutter relaxed, taking his hand off his holster though he kept it hovering just above it.

"Yes, they did. And they shot six of my men. Two are dead, the others badly injured. Whoever they are, I think we are safe to assume they were sent by another tech firm. Meat Co. are the only ones with the time travel science figured out and everyone else wants it. Including the British government who are breathing down our necks and trying to force new laws that will control what we can and cannot do."

"What did they take?"

"Vital technology. They will have paid off one of our own to send them through, but they triggered a silent alarm when they broke into the time vortex generator and accessed the hard drive. We would have caught them, but they triggered the explosion to get away. They'll be back home by now with Meat Co.'s proprietary technology."

"No." Uncle Ralph shook his head. "They didn't get through. The time portal was damaged first."

Captain Cutter absorbed that information for a second. "Well, that's good news and bad. They didn't get away, but we can't get back either." He lunged forward, grabbing the front of Uncle Ralph's uniform. "Now get moving! We'll have to get the time portal fixed, and that's not happening until we get this fire under control."

He started walking, dragging Uncle Ralph with him.

"But what about my brother and his kid?"

Captain Cutter swung around to face Hudson and Rapscallion. Aiming with a big, meaty arm, he said, "Go that way. There are offices there. It's well away from the fire and you should be safe inside."

Instructions given, the captain broke into a jog, taking Uncle Ralph with him.

Hudson sucked some air between his teeth, choosing his next course of action.

"What do we do, Dad?" Rapscallion suddenly felt very alone.

Hudson gave a curt nod, agreeing with the plan inside his head. "We get out of here, son. I think that is the safest plan. Let's find the rovers and leave the building. The smoke is getting bad."

It really was and Rapscallion was beginning to cough as the thick, acrid smog filled the passageway.

Fortunately, they had a good idea where the dino rovers were: Uncle Ralph had been talking as they were walking, and they were parked not far from where they met with Captain Cutter and the guards. Less than a minute later, they exited the rabbit warren of passageways that dominated much of the open-plan base to find themselves facing several dozen specially painted Land Rovers.

Underneath the paint they were just like any other Land Rover, but these were adorned with Meat Co. signs and painted with dark greens and browns in a stripey pattern designed to merge with the background like camouflage. Down the sides each vehicle had 'Dino Rover' written in big green letters. The two O's were made to look like reptilian eyes.

Rapscallion thought it was the coolest car he had ever seen.

If a person had enough money – and that meant millions – they could pay to take a tour of the Cretaceous. Clearly some had because only about half the parking spaces had cars in them.

Muttering under his breath, Hudson grumbled, "I sure hope the keys are in them."

Rapscallion stuck close to his dad as they jogged to the nearest car. The door was open, but there was no key dangling from the ignition. Actually, where Rapscallion expected to see a key there was nowhere for one to go, but that didn't seem to bother his dad who was already getting in.

Hudson stabbed a red button marked 'launch' in the centre of the dashboard and the car's engine instantly fired into life with a growl.

"That sounds like a V8," Hudson remarked, clearly impressed.

Rapscallion didn't know anything much about engines, but if his dad was pleased, it couldn't be anything bad.

"Come on, kid. Jump in the other side and let's get out of here."

Rapscallion did precisely that, scooting around to the passenger side to clamber in. The flames could be seen licking the ceiling now they were facing that way again. He didn't know where they were going to go, and it didn't much matter to him so long as they left where they were. The Meat Co. building seemed strange and exciting when they arrived, but with fire and smoke now threatening the life of every living thing inside, it was the last place on Earth he wanted to be.

Hudson dropped the handbrake and snapped the gearshift into first, pulling out of the parking space and into a lane marked like a road would be at home. An arrow on the floor ahead was marked with the word 'exit' beneath it in bold yellow letters.

Following it led them toward the smoke and flames, but Hudson continued onwards, believing it would lead them outside.

Rapscallion marvelled at the rover's interior. In some places it was just like any other car. The steering wheel and dashboard looked normal. But in the middle and in front of the passenger seat where he was sitting, an array of electronic equipment filled the spaces where an ordinary car would have nothing.

His dad was distracted driving the car, and he hadn't said not to touch. In fact, Rapscallion told himself, it was probably his job as the passenger to figure out what the devices did.

One was clearly a radio. Attached to it was a handset on a cable, presumably so it wouldn't get lost. He hit an obvious button and the device sprang to life, light emanating from a series of dials. It was silent though, which seemed odd given that the building was on fire and the security guards were attempting to coordinate the fight to put it out.

Glancing to the right of the radio, Rapscallion's eyes caught sight of a flat, black circle underneath a clear glass dome. However, it wasn't so much the device's odd appearance that caught his attention, but the words written in the plastic wrapped around its base: Dino Scope.

Rapscallion had no clue what a dino scope did or was for, but the cool name was enough to send his finger in search of an on switch.

Just like the radio, it sprang to life, but while the radio was boring and silent, the dino scope went berserk, beeping like crazy. It was loud too.

A holographic 3D image burst into existence inside the glass dome, dozens upon dozens of dinosaurs appearing. They were all clumped together on the left hand side, each beast with a small line coming from its back that led to a label which identified the dinosaur species.

Rapscallion fiddled with the buttons until he found the one controlling the volume and turned it down.

"What have you found there, Rap?" his dad asked.

"Dino scope. I guess it helps the people taking dino tours to find the dinos. I think the beeping might be a proximity alert. Like it warns when dinosaurs come in range."

"That's cool. Maybe when we get out of here, we will be able to see some more for ourselves." Hudson chose to sound upbeat about it and make his voice sound casual. In truth he was seriously concerned about the fire and the potential for a nuclear explosion. Even if the reactor didn't create a giant mushroom cloud and vaporize everything for miles, the danger of silent, deadly radiation was enough to make him wish they were somewhere else.

Even inside the car they could hear the roar of the flames eating the combustible material and there was more fire on the far wall now than there was even a minute ago when they were getting into the car. Could the guards fight it and win? Or were they already losing?

A cloud of smoke faced them, filling the space ahead like an impenetrable wall. Hudson gritted his teeth, hoping and praying there was no one hidden inside it and honking his horn to let them know he was coming.

Coming out the other side, Hudson sucked in a grateful breath, then coughed, the thick smoke able to find ways into the rover's seemingly safe interior.

"Fans," he choked, punching buttons on the rover's complicated central control panel.

"Drive, Dad," Rapscallion swatted his father's hand away when he tried to help. "I'll figure it out." He was choking too, his t-shirt pulled up with one hand to cover his mouth as a makeshift mask. It didn't do much good, but the interior fans leapt into life, firing cool, fresh, filtered air into their faces.

"Well done, kiddo." Hudson wafted an arm in front of his face to clear the smoke away a little faster. "It can't be much farther. The exit will be around here somewhere."

"There!" Rapscallion pointed through the windscreen. Ahead of them was a wide roller door. It was open all the way to the ceiling, the Cretaceous landscape visible on the other side.

Spurred on by the desire to escape the burning time base, Hudson increased the rover's speed, but a shout from his son stopped him.

Chapter 10

"Dad! Look!" Rapscallion's eyes were as wide as saucers and his head was pressed against the glass for a better look.

The urgency in his son's voice made Hudson twist his head around to see what had him so excited. The moment he did, he saw it too.

Hitting the brake, he stopped the dino rover just a few yards beyond the side passage they had just passed. He hadn't been going fast; the tight confines of the building plus no clue where he was going dictated his cautious speed. Nevertheless, he had to engage reverse and back up to confirm what he had seen.

The hadrosaurs, diplodocuses, triceratops, and other giant herbivores were trapped. Stampeding away from their cages when the alarms and shooting panicked them, they all went the wrong way. They were at another exit, but it was shut.

The terrified animals could probably smell the fresh air on the other side of the huge roller doors, they knew it was their way out, but unless someone operated the switch for them, they had no way to escape.

Worse yet, the fire was coming their way.

"Dad! We have to help them." Rapscallion insisted.

Hudson didn't like it, but his son was right. No one else was going to come and save the dinosaurs. Even though he felt an overwhelming need to get out of the burning time base, he could not in good conscience leave the dinosaurs to die.

Angling the dino rover away from the inviting exit, Hudson sped towards the panicked herbivores.

Coming closer to them, their gargantuan size and capacity to crush anything beneath their feet made Rapscallion question if helping the dinosaurs was such a good idea. They were all so enormous. Any one of them could squish the rover if they stood on it. How were they supposed to get the door open without falling victim to a misplaced diplodocus foot?

Seeing it too, Hudson slowed the dino rover.

"We can't get to the door controls, kid," he warned. "It's way too dangerous."

Rapscallion gritted his teeth. "But we can't just leave them, Dad. There must be something we can do."

An explosion boomed, the shockwave from it rocking the rover. It was another indication that the guards were losing the battle against the fire, and a timely reminder that it was time to be somewhere else.

It also startled the dinosaurs massing by the closed roller door. They trumpeted their alarm and surged away from the echoing boom of the blast, exposing the door controls.

"Dad, look!"

"I see it!" Hudson shouted, his foot already pressing the accelerator to make the dino rover leap forward. They were going to get one shot at freeing the dinosaurs and they had to be quick. "I'm going to try to get close!" he shouted, steering the rover to go around the herbivores.

They were moving toward the door again now, the initial shock of the explosion not enough to keep the terrified dinosaurs back for long.

Rapscallion and his dad were sixty yards from the door controls, then fifty, then forty.

"We're going to make it, Dad!" whooped Rapscallion, excited to be able to save the dinosaurs.

No sooner did the words leave his mouth than he saw how wrong he was. One of the diplodocuses, confused, afraid, and desperate to be anywhere else, turned around, its huge tail whipping an arc through the air. Both Hudson and Rapscallion saw it coming, but there was nothing either one could do to stop it hitting their car.

The tail slammed into the passenger door right by Rapscallion's head. He closed his eyes and used his arms to shield his face, which meant he didn't get to see the world tilting. He could feel it though.

Gravity shifted as the whole car rolled onto its side. Forward momentum meant it kept moving and good thing too because that was the only thing that saved them. The dino rover slid across the floor on its roof, Hudson and Rapscallion hanging from their seatbelts and unable to do anything until it hit the wall and came to a stop.

Hudson grabbed his son's arm. "Are you okay!"

Rapscallion wasn't sure how to answer that question. His ears were ringing, and he felt dizzy and a little sick from being upside down. Also, they were in twice as much trouble as they were before, and he was genuinely scared. The dino rover was on its roof! How were they going to get out of here now? Worse yet, all around there were panicked dinosaurs. If they tried to get out of the rover, they might get squished.

"Are you okay?" Hudson repeated, needing an answer.

"Yes, Dad," Rapscallion squeaked, his voice quiet.

Taking a deep breath, Hudson said, "Well, we can't stay here." He used his feet and one arm to brace himself and take some pressure off the seatbelt so he could get it to release. When it popped free, he fell out of his seat and he needed a few seconds to right himself.

"Hold on," he coached Rapscallion, helping his son to get free too.

A hadrosaur bumped the rover, making it spin and sending both human occupants to their knees as they tried to keep their balance.

"What are we going to do, Dad?" hissed Rapscallion.

Hudson crouched, looking out through the rover's windows.

"We're going to have to make a break for it." He pointed to a space between two of the building's giant columns. "I want you to run for that gap. The dinosaurs are too big to get in there, so you'll be safe from harm."

Rapscallion gripped his dad's arm. "Aren't you coming with me? What are you going to do?"

Hudson nodded his head toward the roller door. "I'm going to operate that thing. With all these dinosaurs around us, we have no safe way to escape. Our only hope is to let them out. That's what we wanted to do anyway, isn't it?"

Rapscallion didn't answer. He couldn't. He knew his dad was right, but getting to the door controls was going to be really dangerous. What was he supposed to do if his dad got hurt?

However, before he could begin to think about the ramifications of what might happen, his dad opened the driver's door and started to get out.

Hudson paused half in and half out of the rover, beckoning for Rapscallion to exit too.

"We're going to wait for a gap, and then we are both going to run. Okay?"

Rapscallion managed to nod that he understood, but he wasn't ready for it when his dad tugged his arm and started running. Almost yanked off his feet, Rapscallion stumbled and had to windmill his arms to stay upright. A shove got him moving in the right direction and a shout from his dad made sure he kept going.

"Don't look back! Just stay out of sight and I'll be with you as soon as the dinosaurs clear out of the way!"

Terrified, Rapscallion pumped his arms, running as hard as he ever had in his life. The smoke in the building filled his lungs, making him cough and wretch even as he sprinted for safety. There were dinosaurs all around, giant legs and powerful tails in every direction. A hadrosaur ran past on his right, the creature's eye swivelling to take in the strange form of the boy racing along beside him. Then it was gone just as swiftly as it appeared.

Ten yards from the columns, a diplodocus stepped into his path. The animal's legs were like tree trunks; too big to go around. But the next leg was swinging into view and if Rapscallion kept going, he could see he was going to collide with it.

Collide with it? More like the diplodocus was going to punt him across the entire building!

He had no time to get out of the way and changing direction would just put him in the path of other dinosaurs. Sucking in a lungful of air, he dropped his legs out from under his body. His butt hit the floor with a jarring crunch, and he slid, scratching his skin even through his clothes as he passed beneath the diplodocus leg, out the other side, and right into the gap between the columns.

"Dad! Dad, I made it!" Rapscallion shouted. He listened to hear his father's reply, but no response came.

Chapter 11

"Dad!" Rapscallion questioned if shouting while surrounded by terrified fifty-ton dinosaurs was a clever idea, but he needed to know where his father was. "Dad!" Was he okay? Did another diplodocus tail get him? Was he hurt?

Rapscallion hung out of the gap between the columns, leaving the security and shelter it provided to get a better look. He coughed and choked again, the smoke getting deep into his lungs each time he filled them to shout for his dad.

"Dad! Where are you?"

Abruptly, a shaft of light appeared at floor level. It was accompanied by a clanking sound, and it took Rapscallion several seconds to realise the light was coming from outside. The roller door was going up. His dad had done it!

The dinosaurs saw it too, their panicked trumpeting changing in tone now that they could see a way out. The door was only a few feet off the ground, but the dinosaurs were not inclined to wait for it to rise any farther. Now that it was moving and they could get their heads underneath it, the giant beasts used their impressive size and bulk to force their way to freedom.

The roller door buckled in the middle, the motor straining to continue turning while the dinosaurs pushed the door outward. In the end there was only going to be one outcome. The roller door ripped free of its mounts on both sides, the herbivores stampeding once more to leave the burning, smoke-filled building behind.

Rapscallion watched it all, unable to take his eyes off the scene and desperately hoping to catch a glimpse of his dad.

The only time he looked away was when he heard a crashing sound. It came from the direction of the dino rover, and he looked that way just in time to see a trio of hadrosaurs bash into it. They were all running to get out of the door, but hadn't allowed enough room to go around the car. Two ended up trying to leap over the overturned vehicle. Uncoordinated, they smashed into it and rolled it back onto its wheels.

Rapscallion punched the air triumphantly. The rover looked battered; barely any of the panels were without dents, but if the engine still worked his dad could drive it and they could escape.

With the last of the dinosaurs running past, Rapscallion came out of his hiding place.

"Dad!" he shouted once again.

"Here! I'm here, Rap!" His dad emerged from the smoke. He was limping slightly, but he looked unhurt otherwise. "Are you okay?"

"I'm fine, Dad." He pointed at the rover. "Did you see?"

Hudson hadn't been in a position to witness the hadrosaurs righting their dino rover, but now that he could he wasted no time.

"Come on, buddy. Let's get out of here!"

Rapscallion started to run, chasing after his dad as he raced to get into the dino rover, but just as his feet got moving he spotted something that demanded a closer look.

In the alcove next to the one in which he had hidden, a small form peeked out. Rapscallion could see what it was – a baby triceratops. Too scared to move, the tiny herbivore was quivering.

Another explosion rocked the building, pieces of flaming debris shooting into the air to rain down around Hudson as he dashed to the rover and clambered in.

He yelled, "Ready?" gunning the engine into life and expecting to see his son in the passenger seat next to him. However, the passenger seat was empty and when he craned his neck to find Rapscallion, he couldn't spot him anywhere.

Fighting a natural urge to panic, Hudson climbed back out through the driver's door, and standing on the seat, looked over the top of the vehicle to get a better view.

Rapscallion's lungs heaved. He was going as fast as he could, but the triceratops, even though it was a baby, weighed more than he'd anticipated. He tried to coax it out of its hiding place, hoping it would chase after the other dinosaurs and find its mum. It was too scared for that though and the human cooing at it wasn't helping matters.

Rapscallion, knowing it was time to leave, gave up trying to make the baby herbivore move and scooped it. With both arms under its belly, he wasn't able to run, but could waddle, so that was what he did.

Rolling his eyes, Hudson dropped back into the driver's seat and got the rover moving. Spinning it around, he skidded to a stop next to Rapscallion, leapt out, and helped his son load the frightened triceratops in through the back door.

Two seconds later, the wheels burned rubber when Hudson stomped hard on the accelerator pedal.

The rover shot through the broken roller door that flapped drunkenly from its mounts.

All at once, they burst from the darkened, dangerous interior of the time base, and into the bright sunlight of the world outside.

Ahead of them, the hadrosaurs, diplodocuses, triceratops, and other dinosaurs were spreading out. They all wanted to put as much distance between themselves and the terrifying time base as possible. The diplodocuses were slow moving, plodding along at a gentle pace, but on two legs, the hadrosaurs had left them behind.

It made Rapscallion happy to see them set free. Truthfully, he never liked that Meat Co. turned them into food for rich people to eat. Sure, they were all going to be wiped out when the asteroid hit the planet, but that was a natural death and somehow much better than being served as someone's main course.

Twisting in his seat, Rapscallion checked their passenger. The tiny triceratops, roughly the size of a fully grown springer spaniel, was looking around the back of the dino rover and looked more confused than scared now.

Turning back to look the way they were going, Rapscallion caught his dad staring at him, one eyebrow raised in question. Seeing it, he risked a guarded, "What?"

His dad jerked his head toward the triceratops. "Thought we could do with a passenger, did you?" He had to shout to be heard over the bleeping from the dino scope. Reaching out, he found the off switch. The dino scope fell silent, the sudden quiet that replaced its warbling alarm a blessed relief.

"He got left behind," Rapscallion replied, thankful to be able to speak at a normal volume. He felt his decision to rescue the baby was completely justified. "I couldn't just leave it."

Hudson laughed and reached across to ruffle his son's hair. In all the chaos and drama, his boy still gave thought to others, even if 'others' was a baby triceratops this time.

"We'll try to get him back to his mother," Hudson remarked, wondering what they might do if that proved impossible.

Now they were out of the building and well away from it, Hudson allowed the rover to slow. The terrain was rough and though the four-by-four vehicle was designed to handle it, doing so at speed was not wise.

He also wanted to get a better look at the time base from the outside. Only when he turned the steering wheel and angled the dino rover so the building filled the windscreen, he wished he hadn't.

A giant gout of flame dominated one side of the time base. Thick black smoke roiled into the air, and it was obvious to anyone with eyes that the building was beyond saving.

"What do we do, Dad?" Rapscallion's question was a good one and it needed an answer. They were not going home back through the time portal, so unless they wanted to stay here forever, they had to come up with a new plan.

Hudson sucked some air between his teeth, wishing he had an answer. In theory they could wait until the fire went out and the Meat Co. people in the present opened the portal from their end. However, with the danger of the nuclear reactor reaching meltdown – they could still hear the warning alarm sounding – staying anywhere near Time Base Alpha was too dangerous.

That meant they had to leave the area. But where were they supposed to go and how long would it take Meat Co. to build a new portal in a new place so they could be rescued? For that matter, if they built a new portal in a new place, how would anyone in the Cretaceous know where it was? It couldn't be anywhere near here. Hudson didn't know how far away they needed to be from the time base in order to be safe, but if the reactor did meltdown and explode, he was certain the distance would be measured in miles.

Reaching across the vehicle, Rapscallion's dad lifted the radio microphone from its cradle. Bringing it close to his mouth, he pressed the button on the side.

"All stations, all stations, anyone receiving? Over."

No response came.

"All stations, all stations, anyone receiving? Over?"

The speaker didn't so much as crackle with static. Squinting his eyes, Hudson checked over the gauge and pressed the send button again. The set appeared to be working, but no one was getting the signal.

"They must have knocked out the base transmitter," he muttered, mostly to himself. It was a sensible tactic for Major Blake's team to employ and the sort of thing they were taught in their regiment. If the enemy cannot communicate, they will struggle to coordinate.

His thoughts were interrupted when Rapscallion spoke.

"How about the other time base?" When his father gave him a bewildered look, Rapscallion added, "The original one."

"That's right!" Hudson exclaimed, suddenly recalling the information from a far corner of his brain. "This is the second time portal. When they first achieved time travel it was at a different place." He racked his mind, begging his memory to supply that which he needed to know. "Nottingham!" he blurted. "It was in Nottingham. They moved to London because they needed a bigger facility, but Meat Co's original time portal must still be there."

He felt like they had just been handed a lifeline. However, Nottingham was more than a hundred miles north of their current position, or would be if they were in the UK. The land masses were different now to the present day and that was going to make navigating their way to it difficult to say the least. It wasn't like they could follow the motorway and get off when the satnav told them to.

Trying not to let the worry he felt show, Hudson said, "We link up with whoever else made it out of there and we form a convoy. We will be much safer together. Then we head north to the other time base."

"How long will that take, Dad?"

Hudson couldn't give an answer. He could only hope some of the Meat Co. staff trapped here would know how to find it.

"Ralph!" Hudson barked, remembering his brother. Ralph was their best bet at getting home and Hudson wanted to know his brother was all right.

To the left as they looked at the time base, people were gathering outside. They were too far away to see who they were, but some wore guard uniforms. Others wore lab coats or suits and all of them had to be Meat Co. employees.

They were bringing out more of the rovers, wisely rescuing the all-terrain vehicles so they too could travel to the firm's other base. Had they all managed to get out though? Were there still people trapped inside?

Ralph's boss said it was probably a rival firm who broke in to steal Meat Co's technology. Was destroying the building always part of their plan? Hudson doubted it since they were trapped here too. Like everyone else, Major Blake and his gang of thieves had to get to the other time portal if they wanted to escape the Cretaceous and suddenly Hudson realised how dangerous that would make them.

In order to get back to their own time, they would have to force the Meat Co. employees to send them through the portal. They must have paid people to get them here, but now it was every man for himself, and Hudson knew Major Blake would kill to get what he needed.

His trip with Rapscallion was supposed to be a fun excursion for his son's birthday. Instead it was a disaster, but if he thought things were as bad as they could possibly get, an ear-splitting roar made him reassess.

Rapscallion and Hudson locked eyes, both certain they knew what made the terrifying sound.

"Dad, was that a ..."

Hudson snapped the gearstick back into first and took off.

"Yup. That was a T-Rex."

Chapter 12

Drawn by the trumpeting alarm calls of the herbivores, a lone tyrannosaurus emerged from the trees. It was already running when it first appeared, but now that it could see prey, it sprinted in earnest.

Out in the open it was fast, and it was coming right for Hudson and Rapscallion. Or that was how it felt to face the enormous carnivore.

Without a moment's hesitation, Hudson floored the accelerator. Concerns for the unknown and rough terrain forgotten in a bid to be somewhere ... anywhere else.

Rapscallion held on with both hands, using one to hold the handle above his head though he could only just reach it, and the other to brace himself against the dashboard. Twisting in his seat to check on the triceratops, he could see the baby was once again terrified - it knew the sound of a predator when it heard one.

There were obvious tracks across the rugged landscape where tourist parties must have trekked in convoys of dino rovers, but there was no option to follow the beaten path. Hudson had angled their vehicle back toward the burning time base, aiming for a gaggle of people massing at the far end. He hoped his brother was there. He wanted to know Ralph was ok, but equally he hoped Ralph might have a plan to get them back home.

Focused on where he was going and trying to balance speed, which Hudson felt was necessary to evade the T-Rex, and caution, because it wouldn't do to crash the rover or get it stuck, he failed to see that the T-Rex was not alone.

In fact, not only was it not alone, it was part of a pack.

When they saw the first T-Rex emerge from the trees, Hudson was swift to react. It meant they were facing the wrong way when six more of the enormous carnivores burst into the open.

They came from all directions, converging on the herbivores still massing on that side of the building.

Rapscallion yelled, "Dad!" his eyes wide and full of fear.

Hudson had already seen the danger, but he had no idea what to do about it. He wanted to join up with the other humans.

They had left the time base by a different door, but his route to them was now blocked.

He veered away just as a T-Rex attacked a diplodocus. The enormous sauropod tried to whip its giant tail to scare the carnivore away, but it was separated from the herd and stood no chance. The creature let out a squealing trumpet of terror as the T-Rex seized it with jaws that looked capable of biting right through its neck.

Rapscallion saw the whole thing and found himself unable to look away. The T-Rex was enormous, at least ten percent bigger than any of the others. There were battle scars on its skin which bore a greenish hue along its back fading into muted browns on its muscular legs. The creature's right arm was missing completely, making the beast look slightly lopsided. Rapscallion idly questioned what animal could possibly have bitten off a T-Rex arm.

A second T-Rex, drawn by the scent of the kill, ran in front of their dino rover, forcing Hudson to stomp on the brakes. It too bit into the downed diplodocus, tearing a chunk of flesh from the dinosaur's hind quarters.

The first one took exception to sharing its meal, even though there was clearly more than the entire pack could eat, and a fight broke out between the two carnivores.

Rapscallion couldn't take his eyes from the sight, staring through the dino rover's side window as his father screamed at the car. The engine stalled when he forced it to stop so suddenly and now it wouldn't start.

Was it damaged from being tumbled and rolled earlier?

Trapped as they were, they were in the perfect position to see a door open on the side of the time base. From it rolled four more of the dino rovers, but these were not being driven by Meat Co. employees. Filling the windscreens, and hanging from the windows, their weapons on display and ready to be used, were Major Blake's squad of tech thieves.

Unexpectedly faced with the pack of T-Rex's they fired into them.

Still stabbing the engine start button with his finger and screaming for their dino rover to start, Hudson saw Major Blake's team cut down the smallest of the T-Rex pack. It had been closest and snapping its jaws at one of the tech thieves' rovers; it failed to understand the danger their guns represented.

Major Blake and his squad were making good their escape, but trying to avoid the herbivores still racing down the side of the time base in their own bid to escape the T-Rex pack, one of their drivers hit a rock. His rover flipped, tumbling across the surface and spilling the men inside through the open windows and doors as they were forced open and ripped off the next time the rover hit the ground.

The T-Rexes fell upon them in an instant, the soldiers' screams abruptly cut off as each carnivore closed their jaws.

For Hudson it was the last thing he needed to see. He knew how precarious their situation had become and how little chance they stood if he couldn't get their dino rover started again.

Two of the T-Rex's were still fighting over the body of the diplodocus thirty yards away, both creatures locked in a deadly battle until one got the upper hand. It was the one with the missing arm that came out on top. It was the larger of the two, and it carried more scars, but the missing limb didn't seem to handicap it in any way.

Biting hold of its opponent, the larger T-Rex threw it to the ground and roared in triumph.

The defetaed carnivore rolled, coming straight for their rover.

"Dad!" This time Rapscallion's shout came with an extra edge of urgency. He thought the T-Rex might roll right on top of them, its weight potentially enough to crush the car.

It stopped short, coming to rest with its nostrils mere inches from Rapscallion's window.

Hudson mashed the starter button again, yelling at the rover to quit playing around and start working. Unable to move, they were surrounded by panicked herbivores and hungry carnivores who were acting like sharks in a feeding frenzy. Anything that came within biting distance suffered a terrible wound and there were dead or dying herbivores littering the immediate area.

"Come on!" Hudson screamed at the car, fiddling with the gear stick and trying the engine yet again. If they were anywhere else, he would have got out to look under the bonnet, but presenting himself as a tasty snack did not appeal.

Rapscallion's eyes were still locked on the T-Rex's nose. If he opened his window and reached out he would be able to pet it. A voice inside his head told him to do just that. I mean, how many people could claim they had touched a T-Rex, but before he could tell the voice it was crazy, the nose moved.

The T-Rex was getting up!

The tiny triceratops baby in the back seat let out a bleat of terror and squirmed backward into the carpet.

With a slight shift of its head, the carnivore was looking into the dino rover, its eyes locked on Rapscallion's. Still lying on its side, the giant beast couldn't attack, or so Rapscallion thought.

Seeing potential prey inside the strange steel box, the T-Rex snapped its jaws, trying to take a bite even as it rolled onto its side and tried to get up. The result was that it shunted the rover six feet forward and three feet to the right.

Hudson had no idea what difference that made, but with a desperate plea for their situation to improve, he hit the starter button again and felt relief flood through his body when the engine roared into life.

Rapscallion screamed, "GO!" at the top of his lungs, gripping hold of his dad's arm even as he tried to steer the rover across the uneven ground.

The T-Rex was on its feet though and the strange thing zipping across the land right under its nose was like a cat seeing a mouse. Instinct kicked in and regardless that he was pursuing a wholly inedible vehicle, it gave chase.

Inside the rover, the occupants didn't need to check behind to know they had a T-Rex on their tail, the beast's thumping footsteps shook the ground each time one landed. It bellowed its excitement, the noise so close that Rapscallion and Hudson felt it inside their bones.

The triceratops, perhaps because it was too scared to stay where it was, squeezed through the gap between the seats and onto Rapscallion's lap. It was unexpected, but not unwelcome, and despite their predicament, Rapscallion found a grin on his face when he hugged the baby dinosaur closer.

Hudson stole a glance to his left, the direction he wanted to be going. The humans who had been massing at the far end of the building were streaking into the distance, dozens of rovers tearing across the ancient tundra to get away from the catastrophe unfolding outside the base. If the nuclear reactor heading for meltdown wasn't enough motivation to get clear, the rampaging dinosaurs certainly were.

He couldn't follow, there were too many obstacles in his path, and it made Hudson want to cry out with frustration. He might have done so too, but he could see how scared Rapscallion was and needed to act calmly for his sake. Besides, catching up to everyone was entirely secondary to their current problem: if they didn't outrun the T-Rex and find safety, they wouldn't need to worry about finding Meat Co's. original time base.

Chapter 13

Half a mile away from the time base and heading north as fast as they could, Major Blake and his elite taskforce were licking their wounds. A quarter of their force had already been killed by the T-Rex pack when they broke out of Time Base Alpha. But they were all professional soldiers and had lost people before.

Nevertheless, losing men was bad, and Major Blake had not expected losses. What stung more was how the easy operation they expected to last little more than an hour had gone wrong from the moment they stole the time travel tech. It was software they needed as much as anything, millions of lines of code that was now stored on a drive no bigger than a finger. It was tucked into the left breast pocket of Major Blake's tactical vest.

Sergeant Hawk carried a spare copy of the same files.

Neither man had any idea what the data they held meant. It was utter gibberish to them and would only be understood by their employer's scientists; people who spent far too much time at school and now worked in darkened rooms for a living.

Stealing the software had been easy. Not cheap, because accessing the highly encrypted data required a passkey and they had to bribe one of the Meat Co. people to get it, but easy enough, nevertheless. However, they were also required to steal the time base's spare time vortex stimulator.

Major Blake was as baffled by the science behind time travel as anyone else, but he knew the time vortex stimulator was the key to opening the portal. Using it, a person could open a virtual doorway to a point in the past or, in reverse, use it to return to their original present. How it worked ... well it could be powered by magic, so far as Major Blake was concerned.

There were mazillions of lines of calculations that went into figuring out how to land a traveller at a specific time, but his employers paid him and his team handsomely to retrieve the spare time vortex simulator they promised him would be stored in Time Base Alpha.

However, when they extracted it from the secure room in which it was kept, overcoming a team of Meat Co's poorly trained guards in the process, one of them triggered an alarm. It was an oversight Major Blake regretted and though he tried not to dwell on past events, it bothered him that he missed the guard reaching for the button on his console.

When he was younger, it would never have happened.

The alarm brought more guards, so despite having some people inside Meat Co. on their payroll, the operation was compromised, and they had to fight their way back to the portal. He thought it to be a minor setback and one they would get away with. Once they passed through the portal to arrive back in the present, they could escape.

Even if they had to shoot their way out.

However, the portal was damaged in the exchange of bullets and now their only hope was to get to Meat Co's original base. It was unmanned, so far as he knew, and abandoned more than a year ago when Meat Co. built their new facility. The original base was nothing more than a trial, a testing station to make sure everything worked and their staff and visitors would be safe.

"Sir," called Sergeant Hawk, getting the boss's attention.

His subordinate's voice penetrated Major Blake's thoughts, bringing him back to the very real situation they now faced. Focusing on Sergeant Hawk, he saw immediately why his attention was needed.

WE ARE NOT MEAT

There were civilians ahead. A party of time tourists by the look of them. Ten rovers with two large, armoured security vehicles for protection. They were parked in the open, the passengers out and taking pictures.

It was obvious the security guards on the armoured vehicles had seen them; their tyres kicked a plume of Cretaceous era dust in their wake that would be seen for miles.

"Do we go around?" asked the driver.

Sitting in the front alongside the man holding the steering wheel, Sergeant Hawk waited for Major Blake's decision.

Major Blake slowly shook his head back and forth.

"No. I want their armoured vehicles. If they send anyone to retrieve what we have stolen, I intend to have all the firepower."

"Won't they be slow, Sir?" Sergeant Hawk questioned. "We need to get to the other time base first, do we not?"

His eyes locked on the armoured vehicles ahead, Major Blake said, "No, we need to get there in time to make the Meat Co. boffins open the portal for us. The security guards will try to resist us, and these fighting vehicles will give us all ssthe advantage we need."

He didn't need to say anything further. The soldiers all knew the stakes. They had stolen Meat Co's proprietary technology, and the firm would do anything to get it back. It was likely the guards ahead of them didn't know about the break in yet; one of the first things they did at the base was knock out the radio transmitter.

This gave them an edge. They were travelling in Meat Co. vehicles. By the time the Meat Co. guards realized what was happening it would be too late.

Major Blake cocked his weapon.

So did everyone else.

Chapter 14

Hudson kept his foot to the floor, pushing the dino rover as hard as it could go and then probably a little more. He was too scared to speak, convinced he was going to hit a rock or burst a tyre.

The T-Rex was keeping pace with them, running with its back level to the ground like a sprinter coming out of the blocks. It was just a few yards behind them, its superior height meaning it could see what was coming far better than the humans it chased.

The rover hit a slight incline, nothing steep enough to reduce their speed or to be worried about until Hudson saw the ground ahead of them simply ended. His heart thumped in his chest, a fresh wave of fear overriding the terror he already felt.

Rapscallion saw it too and gripped the baby triceratops even harder, but there was nothing they could do and nowhere they could go. If they turned to the left or right, the T-Rex would have them. All they could do was hang on and hope the drop on the other side wasn't too great.

But what if this was a chasm in the rock? Hudson's brain conjured the terrifying question as they rocketed into free space.

The rover's momentum carried them up a few more inches, and sailing out into nothingness, both Rapscallion and Hudson got to see how far they had to fall before gravity claimed the dino rover and yanked them down.

Mercifully, they only fell about eight feet, but the jarring crunch when they hit the rock below was enough to rattle the fillings in Hudson's teeth. The rover's suspension did its best, but the impact was great enough to bend steel.

Knowing now was not the time to worry about what damage might have been inflicted, Hudson kept his foot to the pedal and thanked the Lord that their tyres hadn't exploded.

Checking his rear-view mirror, Hudson got to watch the carnivore make the same jump. For a moment, he thought they were doomed, but the T-Rex's right foot hit the ground and buckled beneath the creature's great weight.

It gave a snarl of angry defeat, tripping, crashing, and undoubtedly injuring itself when it slammed hard into the unforgiving rock surface.

Flicking his eyes forward to make sure he didn't drive them into a ravine or off another cliff, Hudson continued to check his rear-view.

"It's not getting up, Dad!" Rapscallion reported, twisted around in his seat to look back at the giant carnivore. He wanted to breathe a sigh of relief but genuinely felt too emotionally spent to manage such a simple feat. Instead, he flopped back into his chair, facing forward again. "I never want to do that again," he remarked, slumping exhausted into the seat padding.

The triceratops looked up at him, its eyes meeting Rapscallion's. He wasn't sure how to read the dinosaur's expression, but it was snuggled into him, and Rapscallion felt a sense of trust or hope coming from its eyes.

Easing one of his hands out from under the infant, Rapscallion, stroked under the baby's chin. The triceratops blinked, but didn't pull away, and after a couple of seconds, it nuzzled its head against Rapscallion's hand.

He'd never had a pet. Unless a person chose to count goldfish, which are fun but not exactly loyal playmates the way a dog can be. His heart filling with joy, Rapscallion hugged the baby triceratops tighter once more.

There were more trees ahead, but Hudson couldn't work out if he was safer to go into them or to stay in the open. In the trees he would be hidden, but he also wouldn't be able to see anything coming.

While he was calculating the best strategy and beginning to angle the rover around to head back toward the time base, albeit aiming for the far end where he'd last seen the Meat Co. staff, Rapscallion voiced a question.

"What do we do now, Dad?"

There were a dozen responses Hudson could have given his son, but he went for, "We get as far away from here as we can. Everyone will be heading for Meat Co's original base, just like you suggested. With the time portal here destroyed, I think that is the only way to get home."

Checking his father's face when he asked his next question, Rapscallion said, "Do you know where it is?"

Hudson pulled a face, exposing his teeth as he sucked air through them.

"Yes and no."

Rapscallion didn't think that was a very good answer.

"What I mean is," his dad expanded, "back in our time, the base is near Nottingham. That's about a four-hour drive on a good day. Maybe a little less. That's on motorways though where there are signposts, and we would have satnav to make sure we got to the right place."

"Satnav won't work here?" Rapscallion questioned before realizing why not and answering his own question. "There are no satellites yet." There wouldn't be for millions of years. "So how do we find it?"

Hudson exhaled slowly. "Well, kiddo, we navigate using the sun and the moon and the stars."

"You can do that?"

Hudson nodded. "Yes." What he didn't say was that identifying north, the one thing he could easily do at any time of the day, wouldn't help them find the original time base. It would take them in the right general direction, but that was all. "However," he added, doing his best to sound confident so Rapscallion wouldn't worry, "I think we ought to find the tracks the other rovers left behind and follow them. If we make good time, we might be able to catch up to everyone else."

"Safety in numbers," Rapscallion remarked, saying the exact words that were in his father's head.

However, Hudson was also thinking in terms of weapons. They were in a treacherous environment where even the harmless plant eating herbivores posed a significant threat. They had a hundred miles to cover across terrain filled with unknown dangers, no means to accurately navigate their way to the destination, nothing with which to defend themselves, no food or water, and if they somehow reached Meat Co's original time base, they had no clue how to operate the time portal device, so unless they got there before everyone else escaped, Hudson couldn't guess when they might be rescued.

Or even if they ever would.

It was a challenge and the only thing keeping Hudson calm as he considered the journey ahead was his years in the army and how many times he'd faced danger before.

Slowly releasing a deep breath, he checked all around for signs of danger and pressed gently on the accelerator pedal. The rover started forward, and now that they no longer had a T-Rex bearing down on them, he felt able to take a little more time and steer a smoother route across the ground.

The pressure to catch up to the distant dust cloud of vehicles remained, but believing the sun wasn't due to set for many hours, Hudson felt confident there was no need to race.

How wrong he was.

Chapter 15

An hour after setting off from the ruined, smoking hulk that remained of Time Base Alpha, Hudson and Rapscallion were still trailing the dust cloud. They were closer, but still some distance behind.

The triceratops baby had been returned to the rear of the dino rover where it had fallen asleep, its crested head tucked against its front paws.

Rapscallion kept turning to check on it, not that it had moved in the last half an hour. He wanted to keep the tiny dinosaur forever, but it was already becoming a bone of contention between him and his father.

"It has to be returned to its mother or its herd," his dad insisted when he saw how fondly Rapscallion was petting it.

"But we just drove away from them," Rapscallion pointed out. "They are behind us. We're not going to go back, are we?"

Hudson grimaced. They couldn't go back. They needed to catch up to the convoy of Meat Co. vehicles and nothing could distract them from the task.

"No, son, we are not going back. Just ... it's a dinosaur, Rap. It belongs here and I get that it is cute now, but it is going to grow ... "

"I know that, Dad," Rapscallion interrupted huffily. "An adult triceratops can weigh more than ten tons. Horny will be twice as big in a month."

"Horny?"

Rapscallion cringed. Giving the dinosaur a name was a natural thing for him to do. How else was he supposed to call to get its attention? However, he knew his dad wouldn't like it.

Sighing a little, he said, "Horny the triceratops. He needed a name, and he has lots of horns."

A rye smile found its way to Hudson's mouth. "Um, I believe we should pick a different name. How about Spikey?"

"Spikey?" Rapscallion repeated, trying the name on for size. "What's wrong with Horny? Why can't my triceratops be Horny?"

Hudson fought to keep a straight face.

"Oh, nothing. It's just that ... it's a cute name for a baby triceratops, but what about when he is fully grown? Spikey is a good, tough name. Much better in many ways."

Rapscallion frowned, thinking through how he felt about the name change.

"Anyway," his father continued talking, "it's not *your* triceratops, Rap. It belongs here in the Cretaceous. It's not like you are going to get to take it home."

"I know that, Dad," Rapscallion's voice bordered on being grumpy.

Hudson let it go. They had enough problems to deal with already, so he wasn't going to get into an argument with his son over the baby triceratops he'd rescued.

Instead, he focused on the route ahead. He wanted to go faster, to close the gap, but had been driving faster than he thought he ought to the whole time so far and his efforts to catch up had almost crashed them twice. The landscape was littered with craggy holes, mud pits that threatened to bog their tyres, and herds of roaming herbivores, each of which he wisely chose to give a wide berth.

Mercifully, there had been no sign of another T-rex, or carnivore of any kind since they left the pack behind at Time Base Alpha.

The sun, which was high in the sky when they first left the time base, was heading west at speed. Hudson could only estimate, but at this time of the year he knew they only had a few hours of sunlight left. The last thing he wanted was to drive at night; it was dangerous enough when he could see what was ahead. At night it would be deadly.

Equally, the idea of parking up to get some sleep filled him with stomach-churning horror. How far ahead would the others be by the morning? Would they stop? Or push on slowly through the night?

With no way of knowing, he chose to increase his speed.

"I'm going to see if we can close the gap," he explained.

Rapscallion hadn't said much in the last hour. Partly this was due to his brain processing all that he'd experienced since coming through the portal. Apart from a fight at school, he could not remember a time when he been genuinely scared, or felt like he was about to come to physical harm. In the last few hours, the possibility of being shot, burned, blown up, trampled, or eaten had never been far away and his mind was reeling. Additionally, in every direction he looked there were dinosaurs and prehistoric plants. It was like landing on a new planet. The Cretaceous landscape was unlike anything he'd ever seen on television. It was a lot warmer too and his dad insisted they couldn't use the rover's air conditioning. According to his father, it would eat up too much fuel and he couldn't tell how much they would need for the journey.

Rapscallion understood the argument, sort of – he couldn't understand how the air con used up more fuel – but he wasn't going to argue because then his dad would provide a long-winded explanation about how the engine and auxiliary systems worked and no one wanted to listen to that.

Wiping the sweat from his forehead, Rapscallion squinted into the distance. Near to a patch of spiky trees growing by a small lake, what looked like parasaurophalus had gathered. There were at least twenty of them. Not a big herd, but clumped together and too far away to be sure what he was seeing.

He wanted to get closer, yet knew his dad would say no so didn't bother to voice the question in his head.

Hudson, meanwhile, had his eyes focused on some dark clouds forming to their right. Coming from the east, a bank of ominous weather rolled in their direction. He could see the haze of falling rain beneath the clouds and questioned not whether, but when it would reach them.

The rain would dampen the soil and that would kill the dust cloud kicked up by the convoy ahead. It might leave behind tyre tracks which would be just as easy to follow, but what if it didn't? What if the rain came so heavy it washed away all signs of the convoy they were chasing?

The worry was enough to make his right foot heavier and their speed crept up by another ten miles an hour.

Ten minutes later, Hudson could tell they were catching up, but also knew the rain was going to hit long before he reached the convoy. He didn't dare to go any faster; it was just too risky. No sooner had the thought passed through his brain than the first fat drop landed on their dusty windscreen.

Closely followed by a second and third, the full force of the downpour battered into the rover ten seconds later, washing it clean and challenging the wipers to sweep it away fast enough.

"I'm going to have to slow down," Hudson announced, keeping Rapscallion informed. All the things he feared, having to find their own way, finding themselves forced to stop for the night, he'd kept to himself. He could see Rapscallion was worried enough without adding more concerns for the almost nine-year-old to consider. Forcing a cheery smile, he grinned at his son. "How many different dinosaurs have you spotted so far?"

Rapscallion shrugged. He didn't really want to talk and wasn't sure of the answer anyway.

Choosing not to push, Hudson peered through the windscreen to the drenched ground beyond.

"With all this rain, do you think we might see any water dinosaurs?" It was a joke of sorts, but one he knew would get a response.

Rapscallion rolled his eyes. "They are called prehistoric marine reptiles, Dad. There are no dinosaurs that lived in the sea, just a few that went for a paddle." He was going to start naming his favourite marine reptiles when he caught sight of something that stopped him. He opened his mouth to speak, but held his tongue, squinting into the distance which was now far darker with the clouds overhead.

When he saw it again, he yelped, "There's someone over there!" pointing the direction with his right hand.

Hudson, concentrating hard on the path ahead and worrying increasingly about how hard it was to see the tracks left by the convoy, twitched his head around to see.

There was nothing where Rapscallion was pointing, only rain and rugged landscape. He went back to making sure he didn't drive them over a cliff.

"Dad!" Rapscallion insisted when his father failed to react. "There's someone over there! They flashed their headlights."

Frowning, Hudson looked again. His son wasn't the kind of kid who made things up, and he was bright enough to know they could ill afford to waste time. Staring through the dino rover's side window past Rapscallion's head, he was just about to look back where they were going when he saw it too.

Headlights, a double flash of twin beams half a mile or more to their left. He hadn't imagined it, and the round lights couldn't be anything else. Momentarily wracked with indecision, Hudson eased his foot off the accelerator and let the rover's speed drop off.

Someone chose to flash their headlights, that meant there had to be someone in the vehicle. Was it the convoy? Had they seen his headlights? Were they trying to attract his attention because they were in trouble? Or to tell him to slow down so they could catch up?

He slowed to a crawl, worried that the ground beneath his tyres might become boggy and trap them if he stopped. Moving at a snail's pace for several seconds, he watched. The headlights flashed several more times. The were getting further away, not closer, which meant they were not catching up. In fact, it probably meant they were stationary and there was something increasingly urgent about the flashes, like they were trying to convey desperation.

Acknowledging that strength in numbers was a good thing and hoping the flashing lights would prove to be part of the convoy with maps and a compass, food, weapons, and all the things he didn't have, Hudson turned the steering wheel and started toward them.

The headlights stopped flashing and came on, the steady light providing a fixed point to guide them in. However, while Rapscallion's excitement grew – he hoped they would have sandwiches – Hudson could feel caution growing in his belly like a heavy weight. Was it someone from the Meat Co. convoy ahead, or could it be the heavily armed soldiers who broke the time portal in their quest to steal the time travel technology?

What if the lights ahead were not guiding them in but acting as a lure?

Chapter 16

The alpha of the T-Rex pack was a fifteen-year-old female. Larger than the males and any of the other females in her pack, she had reigned for more than seven years since killing the previous alpha. She lost her right arm in that fight and had to fight to hide the fever and sickness that followed, plus the challenges from her rivals who thought she might be weakened.

No one had thought to challenge her leadership in years, though she could tell her oldest daughter was biding her time.

Drawn by the panicked cries of hundreds of herbivores when they fled the burning time base, she led her pack to a feast. They killed far more than they could hope to eat and gorged themselves on fresh flesh until they had eaten beyond their fill. Only when it was finished did she realise her youngest pup was missing.

They found him quickly enough, following his scent to the spot where he lay. He was dead, his blood leaking into the dusty ground.

The alpha's brain was basic; she couldn't plan or imagine or perform mathematical equations, but she could see the wounds on her son's broken body and knew what had killed him. There were other carnivores around, species like tarbosaurus and daspletosaurus that were capable of killing an immature T-Rex. But only one species was capable of taking on an adult.

The alpha female had no name for it and though there was one whose hunting grounds bordered hers, they were wise enough to steer clear of each other. She hadn't caught its scent in many seasons.

Regardless, the body at her feet had no teeth marks in it, so there was no question what had caused her pup's death.

Humans.

She had no word for the strange two-legged creatures either, but she knew their scent. She knew the alien, square rock they came in and out of and had seen it being built. She'd even eaten one once, coming across a group of them in the open one day many moons ago.

It tasted very different to anything she ever eaten before. Sweet in many ways, but the coverings it wore over its skin got caught in her teeth and bothered her for days. More than the taste, she remembered the other humans who were with it. They had things in their hands that hurt her. Making loud noises, they spat tiny projectiles that dug into her skin and forced her to flee. Looking down at her body, she could still see the pock-marked scars where her wounds had healed.

Lifting her head, she roared her anger into the sky. Her youngest pup was dead, a member of her pack stolen by the humans and their guns.

Lowering her snout, she sniffed the air, stared into the distance, and started after the fleeing convoy. She was a hunter with a pack at her side and she had a very specific prey in mind: humans.

Chapter 17

"I don't see anyone else," Rapscallion reported.

They were approaching cautiously, taking their time because Hudson couldn't see who it was that waited for their arrival. Friendly or hostile? That was the question.

The rain continued to beat down though its pace was lessening and the dark bank of clouds continued to drift westward followed by clear skies to the east.

As Rapscallion first claimed, the dino rover appeared to be by itself. There were no other vehicles in sight, but the passengers were inside the vehicle, hiding from the rain, so they couldn't see if it was scientists from Time Base Alpha or terrorists from the group who shot their way out of the Meat Co. building.

Hudson's heart beat more rapidly than he would have liked. He wanted to see who was inside the rover before he stopped. It hadn't moved since they started toward it, which meant it was either broken or bogged in.

In turn that meant the people in the rover would need rescuing, but if it *was* the armed men, Hudson believed they were more likely to shoot first and steal their rover than to ask for help.

Fifty yards from the stationary vehicle, Hudson still couldn't see the people inside, so he floored the accelerator. Building up speed and driving straight for it, he aimed to make whoever was inside believe he planned to ram them. If they were the armed men, they would open their doors and start shooting. If they were ordinary people, he would see their shocked faces when he veered away at the last moment.

Forty yards to go, then thirty. Seconds ticked by, but not many of them as he shot across the rain-soaked ground, the rover's tyres sending a wave of dirty water out from either side.

Twenty yards to go. Ten. Hudson yelled, "Hang on!" and cranked the steering wheel hard to one side. The rover leaned as it turned, inertia pushing both passengers to their left as he shot by the other rover on its right hand side.

Both Hudson and Rapscallion stared into the stricken vehicle, their eyes meeting those of a blonde-haired woman in the driver's seat. She looked scared. And angry. Definitely angry, but she wasn't one of the armed gunmen they met in the time base, and neither was the portly man with the double chin on the front passenger seat.

Hudson let his foot off the accelerator, allowing the rover to slow before he prescribed a wide arc to turn around and head back the way he came. Reaching across, he tapped Rapscallion on his arm.

"Quick, Rap, get in the back."

"Huh?"

"Hide!" Hudson hissed urgently. "Just in case. We look like Meat Co. employees," they were still wearing the security guard uniforms Uncle Ralph gave them, "but if these *are* part of Major's Blake's team of thieves, that won't work in our favour."

Rapscallion unclipped his seatbelt, sliding between the front seats to squeeze in tight behind his father's seat just before they got to the other dino rover.

Spikey the triceratops had woken already, and Rapscallion laced an arm around its waist for comfort.

The rain reduced again, the downpour of fat drops weakening to a slight drizzle as Hudson cruised alongside the stationary rover. Swinging around again, he stopped so they were facing the opposite way and his door was next to the other dino rover's driver's door.

The blonde woman inside was getting out before he could apply the handbrake and boy did she look mad.

"What is wrong with you!" she yelled, yanking Hudson's door open. "You could have killed us! I want your identification. I am going to get you fired! This is the last day you'll work for Meat Co.!"

Hudson waited for the lady to run out of steam. Tall and lean, she possessed a Scandinavian look with long blonde hair and deep blue eyes. Her face, arms and legs were tanned, and she was quite strikingly beautiful.

Looking past her and into her rover's interior, Hudson saw the man in the passenger seat. He wore expensive clothes and tucked into the neck of his designer polo shirt was a pair of sunglasses that probably cost more than a car. Of course, to be here as a tourist the man had to be filthy rich. In the back were two women and a girl of about Rapscallion's age. The women had clearly been crying and looked terrified, but the young girl, Hudson realised, wasn't with them, but with the blonde lady.

She looked just like her, right down to the scathing expression she aimed his way. A daughter then, but whatever she was, the people in the dino rover were not the armed thieves from the time base.

Hudson returned his gaze to the blonde lady.

"I thought you might be looking to kill us and steal our rover. We've been shot at, almost suffocated with smoke, came close to getting trampled by stampeding herbivores, almost got eaten by a tyrannosaur, and I guess I felt there was a need for some prudent caution."

The blonde woman's face crumpled. "You don't work for Meat Co., do you?" she cried. "I thought you were a security team come to rescue us."

Driven from the rover by the woman's display of emotion, Hudson slid his legs around and out. He meant to offer some words of reassurance, but before he knew what was happening, the woman had a knife at his throat and a knee against his chest to pin him against the frame of the car.

Thrown by the unexpected change – the lady had gone from angry and upset to deadly and murderous without pausing for breath in between – Hudson slowed his breathing and assessed his opponent. She held the knife with a confident grip. Had she been scared the blade would be shaking.

He registered all these points in the space between two heartbeats and was about to launch a counterattack – planning to shunt the elbow of the arm holding the knife and use the dino rover as leverage as he gripped and threw her – when Rapscallion jumped out from his hiding place.

"Don't hurt my dad!" he begged.

Startled by the sudden appearance of a child, the blonde's eyes left Hudson's. Her attention split and that was all the opportunity Hudson needed.

Flexing his shoulder muscles he thrust his body clear of the rover. At the same time his left hand came up and around. He struck her elbow with enough force to push her hand and the knife it held clear of his throat. The blade nicked his skin, but in a superficial way.

Caught off guard, the blonde-haired lady was unable to react in time to stop Hudson from gripping her other arm and twisting it. In less than a second, he was going to disarm her. Which is why she did what no one would expect: she dropped her feet out from under her body.

She'd been leaning into him, pressing her weight through her raised leg to pin him against the car with a knee. Now she was being pushed back and standing on one leg. But when gravity pulled her down, the man's mode of attack failed.

He still had hold of her left wrist but the rest of her was free to move. The kid in the car was confusing, but she could deal with that later. First and most important was to neutralize the threat the man represented.

When her backside hit the ground, she kicked up, aiming her right foot directly between the man's legs.

Hudson thought he had the woman. Her left wrist was locked in his grip and she was moments from finding herself face down in the dirt. Except suddenly she wasn't there and when her boot drove up into his tender parts, a whoosh of breath left his lungs and he knew he'd been beaten. He couldn't remember the last time anyone got the best of him. He sparred at the dojo most weeks and had taken part in full contact fights without ever losing.

Yet somehow a pretty blonde woman half his size had defeated him and now he just had to hope he could reason with her.

Groaning and sucking air between his teeth while he sagged against the rover, Hudson wheezed, "We came to help you. We're not going to hurt anyone."

Rapscallion threw himself out of the rover, placing his body between that of his father and the blonde lady holding the knife.

"Don't hurt my dad," he repeated, facing the woman defiantly. In his hand he held a tire iron, a steel bar roughly eighteen inches long. Against a knife it wasn't the best weapon but there was no chance he was going to let anyone hurt his father.

To Rapscallion's surprise, the blonde lady looked horrified.

"Sorry," she blurted, putting the knife back into a sheath on her belt as swiftly as she could. "I thought you were the other guys."

The rain, which had been falling still but in an almost insignificant way, finally petered out and in the same moment, the big man finally chose to get out of the car.

"What are you doing, Sarah?" he demanded, his voice loud and harsh. "You said you were going to disarm them and take their car! I want to get out of here right this minute!" He was waddling at speed, and was far bigger than Rapscallion first realized. His face was bright red, and his accent sounded American.

"Angus!" called one of the tearful women from the back seat. "Angus don't get involved! Remember your blood pressure."

Angus wasn't listening, but the blonde lady ignored him. With the knife away, she showed Rapscallion her empty hands.

"I don't recognise your dad," she remarked, looking down at Hudson. "Is he new?"

From behind Rapscallion, Hudson wheezed, "Sarah, is it? I'm Hudson. This is Rapscallion."

Sarah dipped her head in acknowledgment, but said, "You're wearing uniform, but you're not a security guard, are you? Your shoes are wrong, and you don't have a sidearm. That's why I attacked you. I figured you had to be one of the others. The ones who attacked our safari."

Hudson admired her observation skills. "No. We're ... well, we're stowaways, I guess. My brother works for Meat Co. and he smuggled us through. It's my kid's birthday and he wanted to see the dinosaurs before your lot ground them up into burgers."

Nodding along to the explanation which actually made sense, the blonde lady said, "You can put the tyre iron back in the car. I'm sorry I attacked you. Are you okay?" she pulled an 'oops' face.

Rapscallion wasn't sure what to do and the angry American was storming toward them.

"No!" he barked. "I want their car. I paid enough for this trip that I could have bought a fleet of these things. You are going to take us back to the time base. He just said it himself: they are stowaways. Well, you know what they used to do with those? They threw them overboard!"

Rapscallion's eyebrows hitched to the top of his forehead. Was the angry American proposing to take their dino rover and leave them here?

"Priscilla. Judy. Come on, out of the car. We're taking this one."

"No you are not," snarled Hudson, pushing himself back to upright and gritting his teeth against the pain in his gut. It was passing, and even though he was far from ready to fight, he didn't think it would take much effort to beat the portly American.

Angus grabbed for the knife on the blonde lady's belt.

"I'll do it myself," he growled and clearly didn't expect the high elbow she drove backward into his face. It burst his nose and he staggered back, holding it with blood leaking between his fingers.

"You hit me!" he squawked. "You hit me! I'm going to take your job! I'm going to get you fired and then I'm going to sue you for every penny you have ever earned."

The blonde woman shot an apologetic smile at Rapscallion and stuck out her right hand.

"Hi, I'm Sarah Thorisdottir. Sorry if I scared you. And about him," she indicated the annoying American man with the bloody nose. "You really don't have to worry. No one is going to hurt you."

Rapscallion wanted to believe her, but he wasn't ready to put the tyre iron down. Struck by indecision and staring at the woman's hand which she clearly expected him to shake, he was saved by his father.

Hudson pushed away from their dino rover and reached to clasp Sarah's hand.

"I'm Hudson," he introduced himself for a second time. "And this is Rapscallion."

"Rapscallion?" Sarah repeated. "That's unusual."

Hudson smiled. "Yup. He'll never meet someone with the same name, and everyone remembers his the first time they hear it."

Sarah nodded, smiling at Rapscallion. "I bet they do."

The young girl Hudson saw inside the other rover was getting out, clambering over the driver's seat to exit behind her mother.

"This is your daughter?" Hudson guessed.

"Gabrielle," the girl said, sticking out her hand confidently to shake with Rapscallion and then his father.

She was tall and lean like her mother, her head less than half an inch lower than Rapscallion's. Her blonde hair was braided into a long ponytail that hung over her left shoulder and would have been close to waist-length if she let it down. Her eyes, just like her mother's, were like two sparkling sapphires.

Abruptly, Gabrielle's eyes widened, her focus not on Rapscallion or his dad, but at the third pair of eyes peeking out at her from inside their dino rover.

"Oh, my God!" she blurted. "Is that a baby triceratops?"

Rapscallion ducked back into their rover, petting Spikey's head and cooing that he could come out and that it was safe.

"We rescued him," Rapscallion boasted. "He got left behind and was all alone."

Gabrielle rushed forward to get a better look.

"Don't touch, Gabby," her mother warned. "The dinosaurs are wild animals, and their behaviours cannot be predicted." What she didn't say was how difficult it would be to treat a wound if the triceratops, baby or not, chose to bite her hand.

"It's really friendly," Gabrielle reported, scratching under the creature's chin.

"His name is Spikey," said Rapscallion.

The comment caused Sarah to raise one eyebrow at Hudson. "You let him name it?"

Hudson, a little lost for words, said, "Well, I wouldn't exactly say that I let him. We've been looking for some more triceratops so we could return it to its own kind."

Sarah gave a small shake of her head. "Well, you won't find any out here on the plains. No food," she indicated the rock all around them. "They stay close to the forests and watering holes."

The kids were smiling and enjoying the baby triceratops, but Sarah knew they needed to get moving. With a glance at Angus, who was still complaining and making threats, she said, "We really ought to get out of here. It will be dark in a couple of hours, and we don't want to be outside then. We have to get back to the time base."

"The time base?" Hudson questioned. Did she not know?

Beckoning to her passengers, she said, "Come on everyone. We can all fit. We need to get moving."

Blocking her path, Hudson said, "The time base has been destroyed. Hasn't anyone told you?"

Sarah blinked, unsure she had heard him correctly. She was reaching for Angus, trying to get him moving even though he continued to complain and slapped her hand away.

"No, the radio went out a couple of hours ago. We haven't heard anything from anyone since." Her forehead creasing in a deep frown she repeated, "Destroyed?" Then it hit her. "That's why they were going north."

"Who?" snapped Angus. "Who was going north?"

Growing impatient, Sarah also snapped when she replied, "The men who attacked our tour."

Chapter 18

Packed into the rover with Hudson driving and Angus in the front passenger seat because he wouldn't fit anywhere else, the two parties explained their separate stories.

Sarah was aghast to hear about the firefight in the time base and how the portal got destroyed. The news about the reactor leak was even worse, but it explained why they needed to go north. Rapscallion let his father tell the story but felt compelled to interrupt multiple times to fill in parts his dad ought to have told better. Like the bit about them rescuing all the herbivores and almost getting trampled which his dad completely skipped over.

When Hudson described the unit of highly trained soldiers they encountered, Sarah and the others confirmed it was the same people who attacked their tour. They drove straight up to them in their stolen dino rovers. Seeing no reason to suspect anything, the guards the tour took with them did nothing until it was too late.

The soldiers took out the Meat Co. security guards in the first two seconds and it was instantly clear they were after the armoured vehicles Meat Co. used to keep the dino safaris safe in case any carnivores appear.

However, Major Blake's team then fired indiscriminately at the tourists. At the time the tour had been parked overlooking a watering hole where hundreds of dinosaurs were gathered. It made for a perfect photo opportunity. Most of the tourists were out of the rovers, and only due to Angus complaining about the heat were he, his wife, and her sister still in theirs.

It was the only reason they were able to escape. Sarah managed to outrun the soldiers because she knew the land around the watering hole and was able to use a gully to hide her escape. Unfortunately, driving too fast in her haste to get away, she cracked the fuel tank on a rock and once the petrol inside leaked away, they ground to a halt and were stuck.

Angus chose to remind Sarah it was her fault and snapped at his wife when she pointed out they could have died if Sarah hadn't managed to get them clear.

They had been stuck in the car for more than an hour, trying to raise someone on the radio and getting no answer. Now that Sarah knew about the time base, the lack of response from them made sense.

"I think it was one of the first things the soldiers knocked out," Hudson explained. "Ruining communications is a perfect guerilla tactic. It confuses the enemy and stops them from organizing a response."

Sarah frowned, "You say that like it's what you would do."

Hudson shrugged. "It's what I used to do. I was a soldier once." He turned his head to make eye contact with her briefly. She was on the back seat, squished in between Rapscallion and Gabrielle. Priscilla and Judy were behind them on a third row of seats. Spikey was sitting on the floor by Rapscallion's feet, kind of like an obedient dog.

"What about you?" Hudson asked, curious, but really just making conversation. "How did you land a gig as a dinosaur tour guide in the Cretaceous period?"

"I'm a palaeontologist."

Hudson flicked his eyes to the rear-view mirror to see if she was being serious. In his head palaeontologists were all stuffy, dusty old men, not gorgeous Scandinavian women with athletic bodies. He made sure to wipe the doubt from his face before asking, "Where did you study?"

"Lots of places," Sarah replied. "But I did my PhD in Stockholm. They have a great palaeontology program. I was back there, in fact, when this opportunity came up."

"And you brought your daughter with you?" Hudson sought to confirm if Gabrielle was a permanent fixture in the Cretaceous.

"No, she didn't," Gabrielle replied, cutting in to make sure she got to voice her opinion. The way she spoke left no doubt mother and daughter had been arguing about the matter for some time. "I got left behind in Sweden."

"Because there is no school here, Gabrielle," Sarah pointed out, her tone impatient.

Hudson guessed she had made the point many times before. Trying to defuse the argument before it could get under way, he asked, "So Gabrielle is here just for a visit like us?"

Sarah sighed. "She's been pestering me to visit for weeks. She splits her time between staying with her dad and staying with me. I've been working here for two months and it's working out great, but the shifts really mess with my schedule at home."

"I just wanted to see the dinosaurs," Gabrielle defended her 'pestering'.

"I know, sweetie," Sarah gave her daughter a squeeze.

His interest spiked, Rapscallion asked a question about T-Rex behaviour. Fascinated by dinosaurs from a very early age, hence the sneaky trip through Meat Co's time portal, his knowledge for a kid his age was far beyond that which most adults could boast. The T-Rex was one of his favourite carnivores, but in all the books he'd read on the subject, never once had he been given the impression they hunted as a pack.

"That's right," said Sarah, impressed to be offered such a perceptive question – Angus and the two women she had been guiding today didn't even know the dinosaur names. "We are learning a lot from being able to observe their behaviours in the wild. Digging up their fossilized bones is fun, but only because it was the only choice we had. I'm trying to put together a palaeontology program to properly study them."

Angus snorted derisively. "And who's going to pay for that? Time travel costs millions."

"No, actually, it doesn't," Sarah argued. "The research to create the technology and paying for all the hardware cost billions. But Meat Co. have already recouped their investment. Now they are charging high prices to generate additional income because they know idiots like you will pay it." She'd been suffering the opinionated American all day and no longer cared to keep her thoughts quiet. "Opening the portal to send people and equipment back costs almost nothing beyond the staff and power bills. Besides, universities have money."

Unable to keep the hope from his voice, Rapscallion asked, "Do you think they will? Set up a study program, I mean?" His dream was to be a palaeontologist. He also quite fancied being a Jedi knight, but couldn't see how he was going to pull that one off.

Sarah lifted one shoulder slightly in a sort of half shrug. "I believe they will, but I cannot say how many years it might be until that starts."

Angus muttered something about money and having more than enough to not need to worry if Meat Co. had ripped him off. Then he lapsed into a sullen silence, ignoring the dinosaur chatter coming from the back seats.

Hudson drove, his sole focus on the ground ahead. The tyre tracks left behind in the mud by the convoy were patchy at best. The rain did precisely as he expected, wiping out the dust cloud he'd been following, and the rain had fallen so hard there were no tracks at all in places.

Each time the route ahead came into question, he felt his stomach tighten. Were they going the right way? Was there any chance they would find the northern time base by themselves?

He'd checked with Sarah, but as he expected, she had never been there and only had a vague idea where it was.

The tracks, which he'd managed to find again each time they vanished, disappeared once more. It was almost dusk outside and that reduced the distance he could see. That meant if he veered off by more than a few feet, he might pass the tracks and never see them again.

"It's getting dark," he announced, bringing attention back his way. He'd been thinking it for a while and couldn't hold off any longer.

"It really is," agreed Priscilla. Angus's wife spoke with a timid, mousey voice and had a habit of making herself look small.

Sarah leaned forward, staring through the windscreen for several seconds before speaking.

"Head for those rocks," she pointed off to the right. "If we are going to be stuck out here at night, we need to find some cover. A cave if we can. It will be easier to defend."

Hudson wanted to laugh and question what they were going to use to defend it with. They had already confirmed Sarah's rover had as many weapons on it as theirs: none. They did have food and water though, both of which had been thoroughly welcome. Angus complained bitterly about the 'stowaways' eating and drinking rations he'd paid for, but did nothing to stop it from happening.

Memorizing the landscape so he could backtrack to and hope to find the convoy's tracks in the morning when the light would be different, Hudson angled the rover in the direction of the rocks.

It was a cliff or escarpment rising from the ground to a height of perhaps fifty feet. If they could find a cave or even an alcove in which to park for the night, it would make them less visible and limit the directions from which they could be attacked.

They found what they were looking for in the form of a depression in the rock. It was big enough for the rover to be parked out of sight and an overhang above them would keep them dry if it rained again.

Forced to stop driving, Hudson chose to take inventory, inspecting the contents of the rover to see what it might yield. Rapscallion had already found a tyre iron. It wasn't much, as weapons go, but certainly more than nothing.

Strapped to the back of the rover he found a shovel and a pickaxe. Once again, they were not the best weapons, but his arsenal was growing.

"Here," he passed both tools to Sarah, who had come to see what he was doing. "Do you know what else is on board that we might find useful if we have to defend ourselves."

Sarah pulled a face. "Not much. There's a first aid kit, but the tours never get too close to the dinos and we always have the security detachment in the armoured vehicles with us. They have guns and are trained to use them, but I believe I am correct to say they have never once needed to fire so much as a warning shot. The dinos are a little curious sometimes, but generally give us a wide berth. If they ever come close, they drive the armoured vehicles toward them and that's always been enough to scare them away." She gave an apologetic shrug. "We have never needed weapons."

Hudson, who had been digging around in the back end of the car, pulled out and stood up straight once more.

"Well," he scratched his head, "I sure hope we don't need them tonight because what we have won't be enough."

"We'll sleep in the dino rover though, right?" Sarah knew that was the safest option and was going to insist everyone did precisely that if Hudson was foolish enough to argue.

Priscilla and Judy came to stand just behind her, listening in.

Hudson closed the tailgate and took the shovel back from Sarah. "Yes. Staying in the rover is by far the safest option. If something comes our way, we can always move, but I won't want to drive far in the dark. I'm worried turning the headlights on might attract animal life rather than scare it away, and if we are unlucky enough that a carnivore comes along, I'm not sure what the best strategy might be. Trying to outrun it in the car might kill us quicker than staying put."

Rapscallion didn't like their options.

"We should have the dino scope on," Sarah said, while leaning into the rover's cab to flick the switch that brought it to life. "That way, we will know if anything is coming."

Hudson nodded; it was a wise strategy. They probably should have had it on all day, but he'd turned it off in the bedlam outside Time Base Alpha and hadn't thought to turn it on since.

The dino scope lit up from within, but with several sets of eyes watching it, the device remained devoid of dinosaur images – they were in no immediate danger.

Hefting the shovel, Hudson said, "I'm going to look around. I want to make sure there is nothing living in any of the cracks in the cliff face we passed. If there isn't, some of those holes might prove to be perfectly good hiding places. Plus, there will be need to find a little boys' room and a little girls' room if we are going to be here for the night and I for one would like somewhere safe to go."

He made a lot of valid points and did his best not to scare anyone more than they already were. Setting off, he heard a crunch of footsteps hurrying to catch up and turned to see Rapscallion behind him.

"I'm coming with you, Dad."

Hudson thought about sending him back to wait at the dino rover with everyone else. He was likely to be safer there, but Rapscallion didn't know the other people and Hudson recognized that his son would *feel* safer at his dad's side.

"Spikey needs a walk," Rapscallion added, coaxing the baby dinosaur to follow.

Hudson rolled his eyes and stared at the sky for a second, questioning if it was worth pointing out that the triceratops wasn't a dog and probably didn't need a walk at all. He doubted that would work though because the herbivore was already trotting after his son.

Exploring along the cliff face, they spotted a few insects, all of which were bigger than Rapscallion had ever seen before. Their size was not surprising though, he knew the Mesozoic era was responsible for producing many giant creatures including Meganeura, a dragonfly the size of a dog.

However, the cracks in the cliff were devoid of anything larger. No prehistoric snakes or dinosaurs of any kind chose to make homes in the rocks and one of them was big enough for people to hide in.

Spikey found a spiky plant to eat, tearing pieces off it with his beak-like mouth. The cactus looking plant had broad leaves that leaked a milky white juice. Hudson didn't want to eat them, but they looked filling enough for the small dinosaur.

To avoid his son asking to let Spikey eat his fill, Hudson stripped as many of the leaves from the small plant as he could and used them like tempting treats to entice the triceratops to go where he led.

They backtracked and explored on the other side of their rover, making sure they were not parked right next to anything that would appear once night fell to find a car full of tasty humans on which to snack right outside its home.

Satisfied they were in no immediate danger, they went back to the rover. Angus was already asleep, and no one wished to wake him lest he launch a fresh bout of complaints.

Sarah offered them both water, coaching them to sip because they had less than two litres between the six of them and no way to replenish it until they found a water source.

"What about Spikey?" Rapscallion asked.

Hudson placed a hand on his son's shoulder. "We are short on water, buddy. We cannot afford to split it even further to include him."

"But, Dad," Rapscallion began to protest.

"It's fine," interrupted Sarah. "He will get enough water from the plants he is eating," she explained. Taking back the bottle of water, she offered them a granola bar to share. "It's not much," she acknowledged, "but it will keep you going. Hopefully, we can catch up to the convoy in the morning."

Hudson insisted Rapscallion ate it all. He, of course, refused, arguing that his dad needed something to eat too.

It wasn't much, just like Sarah said, but the water and food stopped their bellies from grumbling too loudly. The sun was setting fast and they took a moment, father and son, to absorb the breathtaking view of a sunset over a Cretaceous landscape. Few humans would have ever seen such a thing and with the time base disaster, they could only guess whether anyone would ever return here again.

With dinosaurs still grazing and roaming in the distance, it was an incredible sight to behold. However, the encroaching darkness also brought danger.

"Come on, kiddo," Hudson put an arm around Rapscallion's shoulders, "let's get some sleep."

Chapter 19

Leonard's best people were working on a plan to get the people trapped in the Cretaceous home. He didn't care about them. He didn't care if they were trapped there forever. But he recognised that his opinion would be unpopular and was wise enough to keep his mouth shut when they explained what they were working on.

Far more important matters plagued Leonard's mind.

The time travel technology was revealed to the world with a business plan for million-pounds-a-ticket dinosaur tourism and the genius dino meat industry as the primary drivers. Of course, the world recognised the infinite opportunities time travel opened: pharmaceutical, chemical, medical, scientific ... it really was limitless, but no one had guessed Leonard's biggest aspiration.

He was already richer than most people could dream of being. Richer, in fact, than some countries, but it wasn't enough. He was twelfth on the global rich list.

Twelfth!

He felt appalled by his lack of success and hard work wasn't going to get him to number one. No, if he was going to be the richest person on the planet, he needed to think waaay outside the box, and that was why he had closed the original time base in Nottingham.

Not that it was closed. It just looked as though it was.

The whole scheme had evolved according to his design. He'd conceived the plan long before his scientists actually figured out the final equations to make time travel possible. It was precisely why he ignored everyone in London when they asked why he would locate his base of operation so far away.

Property prices was the excuse he gave, but the real reason was so no one would be watching when he started to steal all the gold and precious minerals from the planet long before anyone in the modern era found them.

The moment Time Base UK opened, and his operation moved south to the banks of the river Thames, he began to use his original base to send equipment back in time. Now dressed to looked like it was in mothballs, no one had any idea what it was being used for. Like a stage magician, he used the brand-new base in the south to keep the audiences' attention focused there. No one even bothered to look at what he was doing elsewhere.

The teams of mining experts he sent back to the Cretaceous were being paid an absolute fortune, but that was the price of secrecy. According to his private accountant, in six months they had extracted more than fifty trillion pounds in gold and a further twelve trillion pounds in precious gems stones.

Unofficially, he was already the richest person on Earth, even if no one knew it yet.

However, the panic that ensued in the wake of the radiation discovery uncovered two undocumented crossings from Time Base UK to Time Base Alpha in the Cretaceous. They were found within minutes of the investigation getting under way, but the controllers being questioned by his specialist team of security experts were all pointing their fingers at a man who was nowhere to be found.

John Metcalf had authorised both trips, logging his name and using his key card to open the time portal each time. Leonard supposed it was wise for Mr Metcalf to have absconded, but the question remained as to who might have gone through.

The huge magnetic field the time portal created made it impossible to have cameras recording the people going through, but if he was asked to guess, Leonard Willis would say it was someone trying to steal his technology.

Everyone wanted it. Not that they would be astute or even brave enough to use it the way he was – to fleece the planet of its finest and most valuable minerals, but they wanted the technology all the same.

He could only assume their attempt to obtain it backfired and their failed efforts resulted in whatever catastrophe caused the reactor meltdown.

A knock at the door broke through Leonard's thoughts.

At the bark of his voice, the door opened inward, three people spilling through it. At the back was Stacey Longbridge, following in behind Jason Curry, one of Leonard's leading scientists, and Martin Fitzpatrick, Leonard's Security Director.

They were carrying schematics and looking as though they needed more sleep, less caffeine, but had recently figured out something exciting which they now needed to share.

"We think we've got it," announced Martin.

Looking pleased, Jason agreed, "It should work, and we can be ready in a few hours."

Feeling like he had arrived in the conversation at least halfway through, Leonard held up a hand to stop them.

"Wait. Got what? What are you talking about?"

Jason and Martin exchanged a glance, both men thinking it ought to be patently obvious what they were talking about.

Speaking first, Jason said, "How to get our people home from the Cretaceous, Sir."

"That's what I told them to work on," explained Stacey.

Not for the first time, Leonard questioned whether it had been wise to keep his true plans for the time travel technology secret from his second in command.

Refocussing his thoughts, Leonard encouraged the two men to continue.

"You think you can mount a rescue operation then?" he questioned. "I thought you said Time Base Alpha was too dangerous to return to now?"

"That's right, Sir, it is," confirmed Jason.

"And we can't just go back to the day before when we know it was safe and get everyone out then?" To Leonard this seemed like an obvious solution, but already knew his chief scientist was about to give him a long and boring reason why they couldn't do that.

"No, Sir. Because of the dual space paradox," Jason looked at his boss expectantly. When he saw the complete lack of understanding, he explained as quickly as possible, "Time runs in a straight line. Once we started sending people back to the Cretaceous, we created a new timeline for them. If we now jump into the middle of that timeline by sending people back to a time before the reactor accident occurs, we cannot predict what might happen, but modular waveform interference is likely and that could create a ripple that would undo the fabric of reality and end all life in our time period before it even came into existence."

Blinking as he tried to keep up, Leonard sought to confirm, "And that would be bad, I'm assuming?"

Jason tilted his head to one side. "All life ending instantly? Yes, Sir, I believe that would fall a fair distance outside of the 'good' scale."

Too bored to argue, Leonard tried to skip things forward, "Right, so what are you proposing?"

"Well," Jason took a step to the left so Martin could lay out a schematic, "the original time base in Nottingham ..."

Leonard's knuckles tightened. They wanted to reactivate it. That was their big plan to get everyone home. They were going to send people and equipment through the old portal – a search team, if you like. They would track down whoever survived the Time Base Alpha disaster and bring them home.

He couldn't allow it, but he couldn't stop it either, not without showing everyone what he was up to. He approved their plan – what choice did he have? However, the moment they left this office, he was on the phone and shouting at the person who picked up his call.

There was a lot of work to do suddenly and very little time to do it.

Chapter 20

The soft bleep woke Sarah, her eyelids fluttering then snapping open. Sitting in the driver's seat she had a stiff neck from sleeping in an awkward position.

Her mouth went dry and her heart beat out a swift staccato beat. Eyes locked on the dino scope, she prayed the soft bleep it just made would be the only one.

As though sensing her concern, Hudson's eyes also flickered open. He was tucked into the corner of the next row of seats with Rapscallion leaning against him. By Rapscallion's side, Gabrielle slept soundlessly.

Seeing how fiercely Sarah was watching the scope, Hudson leaned forward to fill the space between the two front seats.

"Problem?" he asked.

Sarah didn't answer, she went right on staring at the scope. It could produce two different tones, one for herbivores and one for carnivores and the bleep it just gave was not the one she wanted to hear. Not out here in the dark, miles from anywhere and with no protection.

Twenty seconds ticked by, the only sound in the dino rover the gentle snoring coming from Angus.

Thirty seconds. Forty.

Sarah relaxed and that was when the scope bleeped again. It was the same tone as before but this time the scope chose to speak.

'*Warning,*' it announced in a metallic rendition of a woman's voice. '*Carnivore.*'

Sarah knew to expect it. Knew the system was identifying the potential hazard a large carnivore represented. The scope had an effective range of about a mile in any direction. That was plenty of warning to ensure they could move away if a T-Rex or one of the eras other large carnivores came near. That was in the daylight though, not at night when driving was probably as dangerous as facing the predator.

The scope wasn't showing what the dinosaur was yet; it was still too far away, but Sarah couldn't take her eyes from it, hoping whatever it was would just pass by and never come anywhere near them.

Whispering, even though there was no real need to speak so quietly, she said, "It's probably nothing. The big carnivores don't hunt at night. The scope probably just picked up one moving around where it chose to sleep."

Hudson watched the scope too, which is why he saw the blue holographic image of a large carnivore standing on its back legs when it appeared. The thin line coming from its back joined the name above it: T-Rex.

'*Warning. Carnivore,*' the dino scope repeated its earlier message. The blue image was coming closer.

It was still at the very edge of the scope's display which meant it was roughly a mile away. There was no reason to believe it would come their way or get close enough to even notice they were there. However, when the scope repeated the warning message yet again, bleeping softly to remind them there was a dinosaur within detectable range, a second blue figure appeared. Then a third before either Hudson or Sarah had time to blink. They were all T-Rexes and a dread feeling settled into the pit of Hudson's stomach.

"What going on?" asked Rapscallion. Disturbed by his father's movement, he yawned and stretched his arms. His hair was sticking out at weird angles where he'd slept, and he was squinting at the blue light coming from the dino scope. Seeing it, he said, "Oh." His eyes going wide.

Gabrielle awoke too, the quiet sound from the dino scope disturbing her and the two women in the dino rover's back row of seats. The only person still asleep was Angus, the irritating American snoring with his face pressed against the passenger side window.

A fourth and fifth T-Rex hologram appeared. It was a whole pack of them.

Speaking calmly, and fearing he already knew the answer, Hudson asked, "How many packs of T-Rex can an area like this sustain?"

Sarah twisted around to look at his face. "One. The pack have a range of several hundred miles. I thought you said they were at the time base yesterday?"

"They were," Hudson replied, his tone grim. "They followed us."

Sarah's face crinkled. "No. Why would they do that?"

Hudson just shrugged. "We are in their territory and the Meat Co. people have been rounding up their prey, slaughtering it, and shipping it off to the future. Maybe they feel inclined to put a stop to it."

Sarah couldn't tell if he was being serious or not, but now was not the time to discuss T-Rex motivations.

Leaning over the back seats, Rapscallion asked the most pertinent question. "It looks like they are coming our way. What do we do?"

Chapter 21

They continued to watch the dino scope for another minute, but the T-Rex pack was coming closer and if they held their course they would walk right up to the dino rover.

Arguing back and forth in urgent whispers so they wouldn't wake Angus, they couldn't decide what was best. Hudson and Sarah didn't say it, but they wanted to figure out what to do and then tell him, not include Angus in the discussion. However, every tactic sounded just as dangerous.

If they stayed in the dino rover, there was a possibility the T-Rex pack would pass by. In the dark they could be twenty yards away and completely miss the squat vehicle. However, Sarah believed they would smell it.

If they started the car and drove to get away, they ran the risk of the T-Rex pack hearing the engine or seeing the headlights. Sarah couldn't guess if they would give chase; in her opinion they were already acting strangely. T-Rex's don't hunt at night, they sleep. Additionally, driving was risky. Even with the headlights on, the chance of driving into a ditch or off a drop were unfavourably high.

But what did that leave? They couldn't stay where they were, and they couldn't leave.

"We hide," Hudson said it as a statement, like he'd made a decision and that was the end of it.

"Where?" asked Sarah.

"There is a gap in the cliff face about eighty yards behind us. It's big enough for all of us to hide in. The T-Rex's might still find the rover and they might destroy it, but that's the best option I can offer."

Sarah debated the quandary silently for a few seconds, but faced with such poor options, she could offer no better alternative.

Listening to their parents talk, Rapscallion and Gabrielle petted the triceratops. It was on the floor by their feet, but it was awake and agitated as if it could smell the approaching danger.

"OK," Sarah nodded. "We hide." Locking eyes with her daughter, she offered Gabrielle a tight smile. "Ready?"

Gabrielle didn't answer. She'd pestered and pestered her mother to be allowed to join her for a tour – it was going to make her the talk of all her friends and she had some incredible selfies, but she hadn't counted on the trip being dangerous.

Hudson put his hand over Angus's mouth, gently waking him.

"What is it?" demanded Angus. "I was having a pleasant dream," he huffed.

Hudson put his hand back over the man's mouth, forcing him into silence, and offering a warning with his eyes when Angus attempted to fight to get free.

"Shhh," both Hudson and Sarah insisted at the same time.

The other passengers were all silent.

Pointing at the dino scope, Rapscallion whispered, "T-Rexes. Lots of them."

Angus looked too, his eyes flaring in fear.

"We have to hide," Sarah explained.

"Are you mad?" spat Angus. "I'm not going out there! Let's get going. Surely this thing can go faster than a T-Rex!"

"Perhaps it can," Hudson conceded, "but what happens when we drive into a hole or get a puncture because we can't see the rocks in the dark? The second I start the engine, the T-Rex pack will know where we are. There are some small caves in the cliff face. We can hide in those until they pass."

"I think we should do what he says," Priscilla voiced her opinion. So they opened the doors and in a single file they walked back to the narrow cave Hudson found earlier.

Rapscallion worried they might try to leave Spikey behind, but fear that the baby triceratops might attract the T-Rex pack and result in their dino rover's destruction, was enough to make Hudson carry the infant dinosaur under one arm.

However, when they reached the deepest cave, it was very difficult to see inside, and Angus refused to enter.

"I'm not going in there," he argued. "There could be anything lurking in the dark."

"Or there could be nothing," whispered Hudson. "But we know the T-Rexes are out here!" To make his point, he proceeded into the gap in the cliff face, the darkness swallowing him.

Sarah sent Rapscallion after his dad, sent Gabrielle in too, then urged the passengers to follow. Only Sarah and Angus remained outside.

"Are you coming, or not?" she asked as she brushed past him on her way inside the cave. She didn't look back, and suddenly Angus found himself very alone.

He huffed, annoyed that they were all expecting him to go along with their plan. If he'd been given a chance, he would have come up with a far better strategy. In fact, perhaps that's what he should do right now. Afterall, he couldn't see a dinosaur anywhere in sight. He was willing to bet the T-Rex pack had already gone in a different direction.

However, when he glanced to the horizon, the ominous silhouette of a giant carnivore drove a spear of icy cold terror through his heart. Unable to move his feet, he watched a second tyrannosaur emerge from behind the first.

Dumbstruck, he gawped until a hand from the cave gripped his shirt and yanked him into the darkness.

He started to protest, but Sarah clamped a hand over his mouth. From the shadows inside the cave, she had also seen the approaching T-Rex pack and the sight of the one-armed alpha sent a shiver down her spine.

They had followed! Carnivores roam, that was an established pattern for modern meat eaters, but she could not find a reason why a pack would travel so far, especially since they were still moving at night. It was extraordinary. The scientific part of her brain wanted answers ... wanted to see and observe them, but the desire to survive won out, pushing her back into the narrow cave until she bumped into someone behind her.

Everyone stayed silent. They believed they would be safe inside the cave. However, an adult T-Rex weighs eight tons. If the T-Rex pack smelled the humans and found their hiding place, would they be able to break the rock? Would they find and destroy the dino rover? Their best bet was to stay quiet and out of sight, but they had to pray the carnivores wandered by.

"I need a restroom," Angus announced, his voice quiet for once.

"Are you kidding me?" snapped Hudson, his voice able to convey disbelief even in his whisper.

"It's really urgent," Angus whined.

"He always needs to go after he's been asleep," explained Priscilla.

"It's not my fault," Angus pointed out, grumpily. To accentuate his complaint, the sound of escaping gas from the vicinity of Angus's trousers warned the cave's inhabitants of an imminent stench.

"Oh, dear Lord," gasped Sarah, the smell filling her nostrils. She clasped both hands over her face and pulled her shirt up to use as a filter.

The odour distracted them from the danger outside. Until a giant shadow fell across the mouth of the cave. The pack had found them.

Chapter 22

Everyone held their breath. Their hearts didn't actually stop, but it sure felt like they did. No one moved for several seconds. Unlike in the movies, where the sound of an approaching T-Rex can be heard from a distance, these carnivores moved in stealthy silence; so much better for sneaking up on their prey.

Spikey was on the ground with Rapscallion sitting next to him. He was terrified, his tiny body shaking despite Rapscallion's attempts to give comfort, but the little dinosaur was wise enough to stay silent.

Only a tiny amount of moonlight shone past the enormous body blocking out the light, plunging the interior of the cave into almost total darkness.

When it continued onward, Sarah dared to take her next breath, sucking in a lungful of air with gratitude that it wasn't her last. The next T-Rex passed by, casting another giant shadow, but it also continued on its way, vanishing from sight.

The humans could do nothing but watch. The carnivores were unaware of their presence and if they had noticed the dino rover, it seemed they were choosing to ignore it for there were no sounds of destruction filling the night.

A fifth and then a sixth T-Rex came and went, stalking after the rest of the pack. The humans waited, Rapscallion gripping his dad's hand tight for comfort and security, though he knew not even his father could take on a T-Rex and hope to win.

A minute passed and that was all the time Angus was prepared to wait.

"I really need to go," he barged his way to the front of the cave.

"Angus!" cried his wife, trying to stay quiet. "Don't go outside. It's not safe!"

"They've gone!" he argued. "We all saw them leaving. I won't be long."

With that, he left. Priscilla hurried to follow, but found her way blocked by both Hudson and Sarah. She fought, but not very hard. It was clear she didn't really want to follow her husband from the sense of safety the cave offered.

They would have waited for Angus to return, but a squeal of pain from outside changed things. Priscilla barged her way past

Sarah, panic making her voice much too loud when she cried, "Angus!"

Hudson and Sarah darted forward, trying to grab Angus's wife; they needed her to stay quiet. It was bad enough that Angus had gone outside. If the wind shifted, carrying his scent to the T-Rex's, it could spell doom for them all.

They missed her though, Priscilla slipping away from them and out through the mouth of the cave where she turned right to follow her husband's route. When she vanished from sight, Hudson went to chase after, but Sarah's hand on his arm stopped him.

"It's not safe," she warned. "The T-Rex's are bound to hear them."

Hudson clenched his teeth. What should he do? Angus and Priscilla were bound to give their position away. Angus was still groaning and complaining, which meant he was hurt but not that badly - it wasn't as though a T-Rex had got him. But if the T-Rex pack came back, they were bound to find their hiding place in the cliff.

Pulling his arm free from Sarah's grip, he reached the edge of the cave and peered out. It was full night, but where it would be too dark to see much at home, the pollution-free atmosphere provided the clearest view of the night sky he had ever seen.

Millions of stars beamed down and the moon, though no more than a small crescent, provided enough light to create shadows.

Of the T-Rex's there was no sign, so with a deep breath and a small gasp of exertion, he pushed away from the cave mouth and out into the starlit landscape.

Angus was closer than Hudson expected, the rotund American less than thirty feet from the cave. His trousers were around his ankles and he was bent at the waist, his big bottom shining like a giant round moon that had fallen to earth.

Priscilla was bent over examining his rear end, though quite why she would want to, Hudson could not imagine.

"Are you both crazy?" Hudson hissed as he got within whispering distance. "Do you have a death wish?"

"He sat on something spiky," Priscilla explained before, to Hudson's utter disbelief, operating the torch function on her phone to better illuminate her husband's back end.

It lit the whole area, a beam of bright light stealing Hudson's night vision instantly. He swatted her hand, slapping the phone from her grip and he had to clamp a hand over her mouth to stop Priscilla from complaining.

"We need to get back to the cave," Hudson insisted, slowly taking his hand from Priscilla's mouth. "It's not safe out here."

"Well I'm not going anywhere without my phone," snapped Priscilla, yet again speaking far too loudly even though she was keeping her voice down.

"And I need first aid," whined Angus.

Hudson had a good mind to wrestle Angus into submission, but before he could consider the best way to get the American couple back to the semi-security the cave offered, the silhouette of a T-Rex filled the horizon.

Hudson froze, every fibre of his being still as he stared at the dark shape. It was standing on the crest of a small rise at the far end of the cliff face. It was facing their way, and whether it had picked up their scent, seen the flash of light from Priscilla's phone, or heard their overly loud talking, it knew they were there.

"Run!" Hudson ditched all attempts to stay quiet, and chose to abandon Angus and Priscilla. They would have to fend for themselves; his thoughts were only for Rapscallion.

Sarah heard Hudson's cry and was at the cave mouth looking out a heartbeat later. Rapscallion and Gabrielle joined her, worry etched into their faces. They held Spikey the triceratops between them. Illuminated by the moonlight, Judy peered over their heads.

"To the rover!" Hudson shouted, his words a command this time.

To accentuate his instruction, a mighty bellow filled the night air as the T-Rex announced its presence. The roar was so loud it seemed impossible a creature could create so much sound. It made Rapscallion's body vibrate and might have made his feet falter had his father not grabbed his hand.

Yanked from the cave mouth, Rapscallion was still one moment, his heart full of fear, the next he was running so fast his feet could barely keep up. His father had ripped Spikey from his grip and was running with the rotund herbivore under his arm like a rugby ball.

Sarah was right beside them, her long limbs carrying her across the rugged ground as fast as Rapscallion's dad and making him think she could easily outpace them if she wasn't pulling Gabrielle along in her wake.

Judy was left behind, no one willing to wait or go slow so she could keep up. This was a race for survival and Hudson wasn't sure any of them stood a chance.

Their decision to rest up for the night was based entirely on the belief that to drive at night would be foolhardy in the extreme. Gully's, cliffs, rocks, and other obstacles awaited anyone daft enough to try navigating the terrain in the dark. If they put their headlights on, they would be able to see, but make themselves so much easier to follow.

They had no option now though. If they didn't escape the T-Rex pack, they were as good as dead.

"Dad!" Rapscallion gasped as he stumbled on something unseen beneath his feet. Pitching forward, he would have crashed to the ground had his father not been holding so tight to his hand. Even so they had to slow so he could get his feet back under his body and continue running.

The T-Rex was straight ahead of them; ludicrously, they were sprinting toward it. But the dino rover was that way and they could all see they were going to get to it before the T-Rex got to them. Unfortunately, the question of whether they would have enough time to get it started, turn it around, and get it moving before the giant carnivore bit the roof off remained to be seen!

Out of breath from their full speed sprint, Sarah, Hudson, Gabrielle, and Rapscallion slammed into the rover, ripping the doors open and tumbling inside. Hudson all but tossed the triceratops baby onto the backseat.

With a hurried jab of his index finger, he fired the engine into life and stamped hard on the accelerator pedal the moment he got it into gear.

The rover leapt forward, the T-Rex filling the screen as it charged. Worse yet, three more of the pack were hard on its heels, racing to join the feast.

With a slew of gravel, Hudson cranked the steering wheel hard to the right, turning the rover in a circle so tight it felt like the four-by-four vehicle might flip. He knew he was pushing it harder than safety could allow, but there was no choice now. They either got away or they didn't. It really was that simple.

Judy threw her arms in the air, waving them madly as she begged them to stop. Hudson didn't want to. He knew that to slow down to collect the others might result in everyone dying when the T-Rex pack caught them. He also knew he wouldn't be able to live with himself if he drove straight by, leaving her to be eaten as they raced for safety.

Angling the car so he would pass Judy with her on the left side of the car, he shouted, "Grab her!" certain Sarah would have the strength to haul the woman inside the rover without him needing to stop.

Judy had tears running down her face and looked too terrified to think straight, but the very basic human instinct for survival made her grab for Sarah's arms.

If Sarah failed to grip her, if Judy lost her grip and fell, Hudson would have no choice but to leave her behind. The lead T-Rex was less than fifty yards behind them, and it was closing the gap with every stride, going faster than the dino rover as they slowed to rescue passengers.

Judy's frightened cry of desperation ended when Sarah yanked her through the open window. She landed on top of Sarah, her legs sticking out through the window to flail in the air like chicken drumsticks dangled under the T-Rex's nose.

Hudson slammed the gearstick into third and hoped he could see far enough ahead to avoid crashing. His jaw, clenched tight in concentration, was beginning to ache, and he risked a glance at his rear-view mirror, checking to see if the T-Rex was still coming closer.

It wasn't, but it wasn't falling behind either. They were matched for speed and though Hudson could go much faster, he wasn't sure if doing so would be safe and he still needed to stop for Angus and Priscilla.

If he could.

Chapter 23

Flicking his headlights on he found the American couple instantly. Hudson figured the T-Rex pack knew where they were and being able to see where he was going might improve their chances of escape.

Angus had his trousers back in place now, but they hadn't moved from the spot where he left them. Like Judy, they were waving their arms and shouting for the rover to stop, their faces showing their worry that Hudson might choose to drive straight by.

It would have been the sensible strategy. Not because Angus was so pompous and annoying, and not because slowing down even a little bit increased the chance the T-Rex pack might catch them, but because offering the carnivores something to eat might stall them long enough for the rover and its occupants to escape the area.

Hudson debated doing just that for half a second, but like with Judy, he knew he had to stop.

"Get ready!" he warned. With two people to collect, he was going to have to actually stop. Doing so would increase the risk significantly, but he could see no way to collect them both if he continued to move.

With a yell, he jammed on the brakes, the rover's tyres skidding across the dirt to stop with Angus and Priscilla by the passenger's door.

There was no need to shout, "Get in!" but Hudson did it anyway, his bellow echoed by Sarah who shouted for Gabrille and Rapscallion to get into the back seats; they needed room in the front.

Angus showed his true colours, shoving his wife out of the way to get in first. Hudson wanted to kick him out again and make him wait, but knowing that would get everyone killed, he waited until Priscilla had hold of the rover and her feet off the ground before grinding the accelerator once more.

The nearest T-Rex roared, the sound so loud and so close it seemed to come from inside the dino rover. The rest of the pack echoed the sound, declaring their hunger as they chased.

Finally able to focus on getting away, Hudson aimed the car at the horizon and willed it to go faster. The T-Rex was ten yards behind them and still closing. He could see its teeth. He could see the water vapour coming from its nose when it breathed out.

"Dad! Go faster!" Rapscallion yelled. Facing rearwards on the backseats next to Gabrielle, they could see the dinosaur more clearly than anyone. Judy wailed, Priscilla cried, and Sarah held on silently.

"Yeah!" Agreed Angus, his voice a fear-filled shout. "Go faster!"

Heart beating dangerously fast, Hudson whipped the gear stick back into fourth. It wasn't safe to drive this fast during daylight hours, let alone at night, but as the speedometer crept up to fifty, the gap between the back of the dino rover and nearest T-Rex grew wider.

They were getting away.

Ten yards became fifteen, Rapscallion reporting their progress.

Then twenty. Hudson wanted to check his rear view but taking his eyes off the way ahead for even half a second could spell disaster. He'd already needed to swerve around rocks and ditches, spotting them only at the last moment at such a breakneck speed.

The T-Rex trumpeted angrily. Its prey was escaping. Built for short bursts where it would strike slower herbivores with a surprise ambush attack, it had already been running at its fastest for longer than it ever had before.

With the twin red lights of the rover's rear end getting farther and farther away, it slowed and stopped.

"It's given up!" Rapscallion shouted triumphantly.

The report made Hudson flick his eyes up, checking the rear-view to confirm what he desperately hoped would be true.

Of course, just as he predicted, the moment he stopped looking ahead was when he missed the rock in their path.

Chapter 24

The rover struck the rock with jarring impact, launching the four by four into the air. The occupants, none of whom were wearing seat belts except Hudson in the driver's seat, were flung about like pins at a bowling alley.

Cries of fear came from everyone, including Spikey the triceratops who bleated in alarm.

Hudson gritted his teeth, gripping the steering wheel with all his might so he could hope to control the dino rover when the wheels came back to Earth. They seemed to hang in the air for an age though in reality it was less than a second. Glancing in his rear-view mirror, he saw Spikey suspended briefly in mid-air, the dino's eyes finding his before gravity yanked him back down to land on Sarah's lap.

They bounced, the rover's suspension crunching when the full weight of the vehicle and its occupants slammed back into the ground.

"Aaaargh!" Hudson grunted, wrestling to keep the vehicle under control. Again he flicked his eyes to the rear-view, this time to see if the T-Rex's had resumed their pursuit. Did they see him crash into the rock? Would they understand what that signified?

Convinced the rover had to be damaged – he could tell the right front tyre had burst when it hit the rock – Hudson's biggest concern was that they would grind to a halt and be stuck. With the T-Rex pack so close, breaking down now would spell their doom.

He killed the rover's lights, plunging them into darkness.

"What are you doing?" gasped Angus, his voice too loud as always. He reached across for the dial to turn the lights back on and winced when Hudson smacked his hand away.

"I'm making sure we escape," Hudson growled, the tone of his voice a warning.

"You're going to crash again," Angus complained, but he didn't reach for the light switch a second time.

They were going slower now, much slower, but the T-Rexes were not following and despite the punctured tyre, they continued to put distance between themselves and the pack of deadly carnivores.

Hudson made sure the way ahead was clear, then twisted his head around to check the people on the back seat.

"Everyone okay? Rapscallion, how are you doing, kid?"

"I'm fine dad," Rapscallion replied, but his dad could see he was holding one side of his head. "I got a bump," he explained. "When we went airborne, I hit the roof. I'm fine though. It's nothing."

Hudson suspected his son was downplaying the injury much the same way he would. In the military, if it wasn't life threatening, it wasn't worth mentioning.

"Is the car okay?" Sarah enquired.

It was a good question and Hudson would have given an answer had Priscilla not chosen that moment to explode.

"You pushed me out of the way!" she screamed at her husband. "You shoved me to the side so you could save your worthless hide first!"

Angus, his face turning crimson because he knew it was true, turned around to look at his wife. However, when he opened his mouth to speak, Priscilla punched him.

"You would have left me!" she screamed again, drawing her fist back for a second strike.

Angus recoiled though, taking himself out of range. He held his mouth and nose, cupping them as though they might fall off. His eyes were wide with shock.

"But darling I was getting in so I could help you from the inside," he protested.

"No, you weren't," argued Hudson, echoing the thought shared by everyone present.

"You would have left me," Prisicilla repeated. "So I'm leaving you."

It was a bold statement and one which seemed to deflate the poor woman. She collapsed back into her seat where her sister, Judy, cradled her with one arm and glared at her brother-in-law.

No one said anything for almost a minute, the air in the dino rover suddenly uncomfortable.

Finally breaking the silence, Hudson said, "I'm going to stop to check the damage. I think we are safe from the T-Rexes now."

No one argued, and he coasted to a stop. They were driving over a solid, rocky surface of what appeared to be baked, dull orange sand. It had a safe, almost road-like quality provided one could see and steer around the boulders, rocks, and gulleys that pockmarked the landscape.

Rapscallion reached forward between the seats, gripping his father's shoulder with one hand.

"Good driving, Dad."

"Yeah," agreed Sarah, her attention on Gabrielle to make sure she was okay. "I thought for sure the T-Rex's were going to catch us."

Hudson sucked in a deep breath and let it go. They were a long way from being safe, but there was nothing to be gained by voicing his fears. They would tackle each problem one at a time.

The clock told them it was just before three in the morning. That meant they still had several hours until the sun would rise. Time enough to fix the tyre and get some sleep.

Chapter 25

By the time the first sunrays began to peek over the horizon, the occupants of the dino rover were ready to move on. Sleeping in the cramped vehicle's interior was anything but comfortable, and with Angus snoring at maximum volume, it had been all but impossible too.

They decided to leave the tyre until the morning when they could see their surroundings and the task would be safer. Incredibly, changing the wheel only took twelve minutes, Hudson and Sarah doing the bulk of the work with Rapscallion passing tools.

Gabrielle took a turn feeding Spikey, their new location yielding some more of the broad-leafed plants he liked. Sarah identified them as an ancient form of cycad and one that she knew to form a staple part of the triceratops diet.

Off to one side, Angus argued with Priscilla, begging her forgiveness before frustration saw the return of his surly attitude.

"You won't get a penny in the divorce," he threatened.

"Oh, won't I?" Priscilla had growled her response. "Your company was founded in *our* names, remember? Being able to write off more tax was the reason you gave me. I think I will take half of everything, Angus."

"And there's not a thing you can do about it," added Judy with a triumphant smile. The sisters then chose to walk away, cutting off whatever Angus might have to say next. He continued to gripe under his breath and wandered to the far side of the dino rover, probably to avoid helping with the tyre.

The moment the rover was ready to go, everyone crammed back inside it, keen to continue their journey. They had to hope they could pick up the route taken by the convoy and use it to find the rest of the Meat Co. people. That remained their only hope to escape the Cretaceous era and return to their lives in the future.

They drove for a few minutes, scanning the way ahead for any sign of the convoy's passage without finding the tyre tracks they'd been following the previous day. Were they gone?

"Do you think we might have crossed it last night?" Sarah offered a reason why they couldn't find it.

"Was it washed away in the storm?" asked Rapscallion, voicing everyone's worst fears. With no track to follow, they could drive for weeks without finding the convoy or the northern time base. Of course their fuel would run out long before that could happen, and it was already down near the halfway mark.

As things turned out, Sarah was right and they had crossed over it in their escape from the T-Rex pack. Sighs of relief filled the rover when they backtracked and found it.

"So we just follow it until we find them?" asked Rapscallion, confirming what he believed to be the plan.

"That's about it, son," said Hudson, hoping it might prove to be that easy. The convoy might not have stopped to rest the way they had, opting to push on and hoping their strength in numbers would get them to the destination in one piece.

Sarah doubted that would be the case. There was a strict rule about travelling at night: no one was allowed to do it because it was just too dangerous. Knowing they would find out one way or the other they pushed on.

The water supply was getting low and they were almost out of food. Rapscallion's stomach gurgled and grumbled its emptiness, but he kept quiet knowing everyone else was in exactly the same situation.

Hudson drove for a while before swapping with Sarah. She was more experienced and more familiar with the terrain though they were already way outside the area she usually travelled.

Just over an hour into their journey they stopped for a bathroom break, taking it in turns to go behind some rocks while the others kept a lookout, though Sarah assured everyone the likelihood of encountering a carnivore was slim.

Waiting for his dad, who went last, Rapscallion asked Sarah a question. "You said the T-Rex pack hunting at night was unusual."

"Really unusual," she agreed.

"So why were they doing it?"

Sarah sucked some air between her teeth. "It might be that they were not hunting at all. It could be that something else made them decide to leave their previous hunting ground."

"Like what?" Rapscallion couldn't imagine why a pack of carnivores would leave such a plentiful feeding area; there had been herbivores in every direction.

"Another predator moving in would do it."

Rapscallion's brow wrinkled in confusion. "What could possibly make a T-Rex pack decide to move out. They are the apex predators."

"Ah," Sarah nodded. "Actually, they are not. At least I don't think so."

Now Rapscallion was all ears. Something that was bigger, badder, and scarier than T-Rex?

"I haven't seen it yet and neither has anyone else, but we found a set of footprints. They are roughly thirty percent bigger than the biggest T-Rex and it walks on all four feet. I want to study it. I mean, that's an obvious thing to say for a palaeontologist, and there is so much here to study, but finding and naming a huge carnivore would capture the public imagination back home and attract funding I could use to bring more scientists back here. The potential secrets locked in this time zone are unimaginable. The cure for cancer could be here."

"Ready?" asked Rapscallion's dad, reappearing from behind the rocks.

Rapscallion was about to give his dad a thumbs up when a volley of gunfire echoed through the air.

Chapter 26

There could be no mistaking the sound and the only good thing to note was how far away it sounded – whoever they were shooting at, it wasn't Hudson, Rapscallion, and their party.

Sarah and Hudson's eyes met.

"That's gotta be the convoy!" They said it at exactly the same time and with the exact same amount of excitement.

"Ha! Jinx!" laughed Rapscallion, but his comment seemed to go unheard by everyone but Gabrielle. Sarah and Hudson were looking at each other, something unsaid passing between them.

"Come on, kiddo! Let's go!" Hudson ushered Rapscallion toward the rover, shouting, "Everyone in!" to make sure the rest of their party were on board.

"I'll drive!" shouted Sarah, racing to get to the driver's door only to have Hudson beat her to it. She slapped his arm grumpily. "No fair. You get to drive all the time."

"Sorry," he laughed, fending off her blows, "I got here first. Besides, this is my rover," he teased, "You killed yours, remember?"

Judy and Priscilla were already inside, the two ladies volunteering to take the back row, probably to be as far away from Angus as possible. Gabrielle and Rapscallion happily took the middle row, positioning themselves with a gap in the middle for Sarah.

Rapscallion gave Sarah enough time to swing into her space, then yelled, "Punch it!" at his father, his excitement bubbling over now that they thought they might catch up to the convoy.

They set off at speed, racing across the open countryside for it was daylight and they could see for miles now. The rocky, rugged terrain was behind them and ahead they could see flat plains. Tufts of green vegetation sprouted in patches, but looking from his window, it was nothing like the grass or tender-stemmed plants Rapscallion was used to seeing in his garden. They were spiky and hardy looking instead. More like cactus in fact.

Ahead there were mountains, but even though they looked tall, there was no snow on top. Rapscallion wondered if that might be because the planet was so much warmer now than in their own time. At the base of the mountains and about halfway up the sides, they were lusciously green. In fact much of the landscape was covered in forest, the Cretaceous plants growing rampant despite the herds of huge herbivore who must be able to eat their way through a sizeable woodland every day.

A plume of dust arose in their wake, pulled from the ground by the air turbulence caused by their speed. Hudson hoped it might be seen by someone, anyone in the convoy. If they could see someone coming they might slow, or leave a few vehicles behind to wait for them.

"What do you think they were shooting at?" Hudson asked, twisting his neck to look at Sarah when he posed the question.

She shrugged in an exaggerated way. "Could be predators. Maybe they needed food and chose to kill a small herbivore," she hedged a guess.

"Maybe it was the same bunch that attacked us," muttered Angus.

His words made everyone fall silent. Hudson had all but forgotten the dinosaurs and the terrain were not the only dangers they faced. The last thing he wanted to do was run into Major Blake's armed gunmen again. They were dangerous and desperate, and he wanted to avoid them at all costs.

Inside the dino rover it was impossible to hear if there had been any further gunshots, so Hudson slowed their pace and opened his window. However, when he did so, what he heard was not a volley of shots like before, but a full-blown gun battle just like they faced back in Time Base Alpha.

Taking a deep breath to steady himself, he questioned what that could mean.

"Dad?" Rapscallion called to get his father's attention.

"Yes, son?"

"That's another battle, isn't it?"

Hudson nodded. "Yes, Rap, I believe it is." He flicked his eyes up to look in the rear-view mirror hoping to catch his son's gaze but finding Sarah's eyes instead. They exchanged a worried glance.

They knew Major Blake's team of tech thieves had taken the armoured fighting vehicles from the safari tour. He would have bet on Major Blake's men over the Meat Co. security guards any day of the week. Adding armoured vehicles to their armoury meant they would be invincible.

"Look, there!" cried Judy, jabbing an arm between the front seats.

The suddenness of her move, especially from a woman who said nothing ninety-nine percent of the time, made Hudson jump, but he saw what she was pointing at, and it sent a warm feeling through his entire body.

There is one thing a soldier learns very early on in training: to look for that which does not belong. Finding the enemy when they are hiding in the trees is no easy thing, but movement will give them away every time. So will noise and so will shape.

It was shape they were seeing now. Very few things in nature create straight lines and that was what they could see ahead of them. It was still in the distance; at least a mile away if not closer to two, but they were looking at the vehicles in the Meat Co. convoy and they had stopped moving, which made them easy to spot.

In fact, now they were seeing them, they were impossible to miss.

Their dino rover was still following the tracks the convoy left behind and it was going to take them straight to it. Hudson wanted to feel jubilant. Truthfully, he did, but he was also confused.

"The shooting isn't coming from the convoy," said Sarah, leaning through from the backseats. In voicing her thoughts she perfectly captured the thing that most bothered Hudson.

"What does that mean, Dad?" Rapscallion squeezed under Sarah's arm to get a better look.

Hudson swallowed before he answered, knowing what he believed it meant and not liking it one little bit.

"It means there is trouble ahead."

Chapter 27

They caught up to the convoy faster than they expected. Coming closer, they saw guns pointing their way, the Meat Co. security guards cautious of the vehicle heading for them.

To allay their suspicions and hopefully avoid getting shot, they wound down all the rover's windows and hung their arms out to show they were not holding weapons.

Hudson approached slowly and when they were within shouting distance, he stopped and got out. Sarah, Angus, and everyone else got out too.

"From the tour group," Sarah shouted. "We got separated."

That appeared to be all the explanation the Meat Co. security required. They lowered their guns and waved the late arrivals forward where they were met by the senior person in charge.

"That's Robert Banks," Sarah whispered, leaning her head toward Hudson, though Rapscallion was close enough to hear what she said. "He's one of the firm's Senior Vice Presidents and the top man out here in the Cretaceous."

"Sarah?" Mr Banks sounded relieved to see her. "Oh, my goodness. I'm so glad to see you are all right."

"What about us?" snapped Angus. "Nevermind the pretty blonde woman. We're the customers. We're the ones who paid to be here! It's outrageous. I've a good mind to ..."

"Oh, shut up, Angus," Priscilla cut him off mid-sentence. "No one cares what you think." Turning her attention to the man in charge, she asked, "Do you have any food? Everyone is rather hungry and we have two children in our party."

"Hungry?" muttered Angus. "More like starving."

A young woman wearing office clothes – hardly the outfit for a day in the Cretaceous wastelands, beckoned Priscilla to follow her. She did so, arm in arm with Judy, leaving Angus to trail grumpily behind.

When they passed Robert Banks, he watched them go but swiftly turned his attention back to Sarah.

"You're not hurt?"

"No, I'm fine," she replied, her tone dismissing his concerns. "Did the rest of our tour already find you?"

"Yes," Robert nodded. "That was yesterday afternoon, not long after the attack happened. I sent some guards to look for you, but they found no sign."

Sarah didn't want to get into the details of what happened; they could do that later when they were all safe in their own time period. Instead she said, "Our dino rover got damaged in our escape, but we were lucky enough to be found by these gentlemen." She indicated Hudson and Rapscallion. "Thank you for waiting so we could catch up. We heard shooting."

Tugging lightly at his father's shirt, Rapscallion whispered, "Where's Uncle Ralph? I can't see him."

Hudson felt he had waited long enough to speak. His hope that Ralph would be here with the convoy was fading. His brother hadn't come forward and scanning the vehicles and people milling about, there was no sign of him.

Demanding answers, he said, "Mr Banks I'm Hudson Gilbert. This is my son Rapscallion. My brother is one of your security guards. Ralph Gilbert. Is he here? Did he get out of Time Base Alpha?"

A slight frown creased Robert Banks' brow, but he didn't give an answer. Not straight away at least. Instead, he turned to his left and motioned for a man in Meat Co. security guard clothing.

Hudson recognised him instantly – it was Captain Cutter, the man who separated them from Uncle Ralph back at the time base. The last time Hudson saw his brother he was running through the base to tackle the fire. That was almost a day ago now.

"Cutter, where is Ralph Gilbert? Is he with the convoy?" The worry in Robert's voice made Rapscallion fear the worst. Did his uncle get left behind at the base? Had something terrible befallen him in the chaos of the T-Rex attack?

Captain Cutter eyed Hudson and Rapscallion, his expression anything but friendly. "Sir, this man and his son are stowaways. Gilbert snuck them through the time portal for a little excursion."

"That's hardly relevant, Cutter."

"But look at the state of their dino rover, Sir. It's destroyed. They are responsible for that damage."

He wasn't wrong, the dino rover didn't look good. The spare tyre was wrecked, almost every panel on the vehicle was dented, including the roof, and the front bumper was hanging off a bit.

Dismissing Captain Cutter's concerns, Robert Banks said, "Right now the focus is on survival and getting everyone home. Recriminations and investigations can come later." The boss man's response shot Captain Cutter down in an instant. "Now, where is Ralph Gilbert?"

"I sent him with the fighting party. They went after the thieves, just like you ordered."

The news struck Hudson like a wave of cold water to the face. "You sent your security guards up against Major Blake and his men?" He couldn't believe it.

"They have our technology," Robert Banks defended his actions. "If they make it back to the present, they could ruin Meat Co. We have more than five thousand employees depending on us, not to mention the stakeholders who invested in the firm. We have to get it back at all costs. When we spotted them an hour ago, I had no choice but to send our best troops to intercept."

His voice a low growl, Hudson snarled, "But they are not troops at all. They are security guards. Poorly trained ones at that and you just sent them up against elite soldiers. They won't stand a chance."

As if to punctuate his statement, a volley of gunfire ripped through the air again, the sound bouncing off the distant mountains. It was returned by more and a full-blown gun battle broke out once more.

Hudson turned his body to face the direction it came from.

"That's close," he said, the remark aimed only at himself. "Less than a mile."

Rapscallion, worried for his uncle, but equally concerned about what his dad might do now, took his father's hand.

Hudson twisted to face his son and crouched so their heads were the same level.

"I have to go help your uncle, Rap. I want you to stay here with Sarah and Gabrielle. I'll be back as soon as I can."

"No one is going anywhere," argued Captain Cutter.

His face hardening, Hudson narrowed his eyes at Meat Co's head of security. "Some leader you are. You should be with them, facing the same danger. I'm going and that's final."

"Everyone, please just calm down," Mr Banks tried to deescalate the situation. Holding an electronic tablet aloft, he said, "The reactor is still getting hotter. We are probably far enough away now, but we really should keep moving. When the core reaches critical mass, it will explode, just like a nuclear bomb."

The device showed a bunch of graphs and readings. Hudson couldn't see what they showed and cared even less. Yes, they probably should keep moving, but not without his brother.

Turning his back on Cutter and Banks, he started back to his battered dino rover. To his way of thinking, there was no time to lose. Discussing what course of action to take would eat up precious seconds and he wasn't inclined to listen to anyone when he already knew what needed to be done. The security guards had been sent to take on a team of special forces soldiers and they were going to lose. Hudson wasn't going to turn the tide and win the battle; he didn't even have a gun, but he certainly wasn't going to sit around and wait to see if his brother came back alive.

Captain Cutter had other ideas. Producing his handgun from the holster on his hip, he aimed it at Hudson.

"That dino rover is the property of Meat Co. You are not taking it anywhere."

"Don't shoot my dad!" Rapscallion shouted a panicked cry.

Seeing their boss and the head of security arguing with a man and a boy they didn't recognise, more of the Meat Co. personnel were drifting to the rear of the convoy where Hudson and Captain Cutter were facing off.

Tuning out Rapscallion's anguished cries, Hudson stalked toward the head of security. The man had a gun pointing straight at him, but if that scared Rapscallion's father, he showed no sign.

"I'm warning you," Cutter barked.

Robert and Sarah were both trying to calm things down, urging Captain Cutter to put the weapon away.

"Warning me?" Hudson questioned. "Warning me about what?" He asked the question, looking directly into Captain Cutter's eyes for a reaction. The gun was pointing at his chest, less than a foot from his shirt. If Cutter pulled the trigger there was no chance he could miss.

However, in a blur of movement so fast the human eye would struggle to track it, Hudson jerked to his right and went forward, closing the distance between the two men. His right arm whipped upward and as his body came clear of the gun's muzzle, he ripped it from Captain Cutter's grip.

He was spinning by this point, the handgun now in his possession. Backing into Cutter's side, he aimed a fast left elbow to his ribs, ducked under his flailing arms and kicked out his knees from behind.

Rapscallion knew his father was a good martial artist and had served in the special forces so was comfortable around guns, but he'd never seen anyone move so fast or disarm someone so easily, not even on TV.

Cutter fell to the ground with Rapscallion's father standing over him.

Hudson checked the weapon, ejecting the magazine to confirm it was full before pocketing it in his jeans.

"I'm going after my brother," he repeated, the iron-hard firmness with which he delivered the statement leaving no room for argument.

When his father started toward the rover once more, Rapscallion raced after him.

"I want to go with you, Dad."

"I'm coming too," said Sarah which really left no room for Hudson to argue. There wasn't time either and truthfully he felt safer knowing where his son was.

"Okay then," Hudson clambered into the rover. "Let's go get Uncle Ralph."

Chapter 28

To the west, a different set of ears tracked the sound of gunfire. The T-Rex alpha was tired and her pack wanted to rest, but her brain had room for no emotion other than hatred.

When they stumbled across the humans in the middle of the night, her excitement had been palpable. She wanted to kill them, to end their ability to fight back with their strange, noise-making sticks. They had killed her child and she was determined to be certain that could never happen again.

However, the humans last night were not the ones she wanted. Oh, she would have killed every one of them and feasted on their puny bodies if she'd gotten the chance, but they didn't shoot at her pack, so they were not the ones responsible for her pup's death.

Everything about the humans was alien and she hated it, so when she heard the now familiar sound of the humans firing their guns, she bellowed a roar to get her pack moving.

WE ARE NOT MEAT

It was time to hunt.

Chapter 29

They peeled away from the rear of the convoy in a plume of dust, the rover's tyres kicking up the soft dusty dirt when Hudson floored the accelerator. The windows were still open, but that meant they could hear the battle more clearly.

It was still raging, rattles of machinegun fire filling the quiet air like a million angry party poppers. To Rapscallion it seemed mad that they were driving toward the battle instead of away, but if his dad said they needed to rescue Uncle Ralph, he wasn't going to argue.

Spikey the triceratops leaned against his leg. Rapscallion chose to hide him when they caught up to the convoy, believing the adults would be too preoccupied to notice. He was worried the Meat Co. people might make him leave the baby dino behind and he wasn't prepared to do that. Truthfully, he wanted to take Spikey home to keep as a pet, but knew that was never going to happen. Instead, he would be satisfied to know his little friend was somewhere safe when they departed.

Just two minutes after setting off, they spotted smoke rising into the air. Something was on fire ahead. It gave them a focal point to aim for, but Hudson slowed as they came closer.

"What do we do?" asked Sarah, her voice edged with worry. "We can't just drive straight into the middle of the fight, surely."

Hudson pointed. "I'm heading for that high ground. It might give us a view of the battleground and I think those rocks will give us some cover."

Rapscallion could see where his dad meant. They were coming into another rocky region, the ground rising and falling with rock formations creating sharp rises and gulleys. Among them, giant Cretaceous trees grew abundantly, forming a forest that looked so dense they would never get the rover through it.

Hudson pulled up behind a sharply angled outcropping of rocks and almost before the rover stopped moving he was out and scaling the rocks, pausing only long enough to say, "Wait here," before disappearing.

"Wait here?" Sarah repeated. "I don't think so. Come on, kids. Rapscallion, you need to point your uncle out to us if you see him."

Rapscallion flicked a glance at Gabrielle. He was oddly excited to be so close to a battle and hardly scared at all.

"Stay here," he coached Spikey, leaving the triceratops behind when he closed the dino rover's door.

With Sarah leading, they all clambered up the rocks after Rapscallion's dad, keeping low. Ahead of them, Hudson reached the top and peered over. His concentration focused on the scene ahead, it was only when Sarah reached his side that he noticed he wasn't alone.

"I told you to stay in the rover."

Sarah showed him a raised eyebrow. She wasn't used to taking orders from anyone and wasn't about to start.

"The kids too?" Hudson complained as Gabrielle and Rapscallion joined them.

All four peeked over the brow of the ridge, but whatever it was they expected to see, the scene below wasn't it.

One of the two armoured personnel carriers Major Blake's soldiers took was stuck in a bog, the front axle almost completely submerged. It would take a large recovery vehicle with a strong winch to get it out and knowing this they had already abandoned it.

They were using it for cover as they fired at the Meat Co. security guards. Using the .50 Cal mounted on the armoured vehicle's roof they were having no trouble controlling the battle.

Hudson couldn't see his brother, but the Meat Co. uniforms were easy to spot. They had chased Major Blake's team of thieves using dino rovers, hardly a match for the armoured vehicles and their superior weapons. Two of the rovers were on fire – the source of the smoke Hudson used to find the battle's location – and at least two more had been shot to pieces. One was on its side, the windscreen smashed and a tyre punctured where the driver had lost control.

The bulk of the Meat Co. guys were hunkered down behind some more rocks where two more of the rovers were parked.

What was instantly clear to Hudson was their lack of organisation. The soldiers at the bogged vehicle were laying down suppressing fire with their guns, keeping the Meat Co. team pinned down. Any attempt to move forward out of the small gulley in which they hid would put them directly in the line of fire and likely get them killed.

Meanwhile, the rest of Major Blake's soldiers were winding their way around from the east using the trees for cover. Hudson could see them because he was above the battle, but he was willing to bet the Meat Co. guys had no idea they were about to get ambushed. If they stayed where they were the team of thieves would slaughter them.

"Uncle Ralph must be down there," Hudson angled a hand at the gaggle of security guards. "But they are about to be attacked." He grabbed Sarah's arm. "Get back to the rover and take it around to the back of those trees." Hudson pointed to a small copse fifty yards behind the security guards. "I'll meet you there."

With a grunt of effort, Hudson pushed himself up, being extra careful not to show his head above the ridge and give away his position. What he intended to do would only work if Major Blake and his men had no idea he was there.

Sarah snatched hold of his arm to stop him. "What are you going to do?"

Hudson huffed out a hard breath. "Whatever I can."

Chapter 30

Hudson slipped and slid down the steep rocky slope, calling back over his shoulder, "Just be ready and keep the engine running. We may need to make a fast getaway."

Sarah didn't doubt that for a moment. With Hudson heading right to go around the rocks, in the opposite direction to where the Meat Co. security guards were pinned down, she made a beeline back to the rover.

However, when she got there, thinking the kids were right on her heels, she found herself alone.

"Gabrielle!" she yelled, trying hard to not shout too loud, but needing to know where her daughter could have gone. "Rapscallion!" Hudson's son had gone too, and she could guess where: they had followed Rapscallion's dad instead of doing what they were told.

Hudson ran, keeping low. He didn't want to shoot anyone. The truth was that all he wanted to do was find a way to get back to their own time zone and stay there forever. But his brother was in trouble and helping him had to happen first. Ralph could quit his job with Meat Co. when they got back to the present. Or not. The point was to make sure he had the chance to make a choice, not to let him die here in the Cretaceous.

Slowing his pace, Hudson stopped to listen. The thieves at the bogged vehicle were still shooting, the sound loud enough to make hearing anything else difficult, but he knew the other half of their force would be coming his way any moment now. Their route to get around behind the Meat Co. team would lead them through a gap between the rocks. He only had a handgun, but they wouldn't be expecting him and that gave him a big advantage.

The trees rustled, the passage of Major Blake's men making the branches move. They were coming to him. All Hudson needed to do was stay low and wait for the right moment.

Of course, the moment he thought that, he saw something that sent a terrifying chill through his entire body.

Chapter 31

"Do you see him?" Gabrielle asked, her voice a nervous whisper.

Rapscallion almost went with Sarah to the rover, but he wanted to help his dad and in this environment it made him nervous to be separated from him.

He shook his head. "No." Gabrielle wasn't supposed to have followed him. He expected her to go with her mum, but by the time he realised she was still with him it was too late to turn back.

"What do we do?"

Rapscallion wanted to have a decisive answer, just like his dad would. His dad always knew what to do and was never flustered. Rapscallion chose to quell his rising nerves and pretend he had it all under control.

"We push on. He won't be far ahead." They were among the rocks, no longer on the high ground where they might have seen the threat approaching.

They didn't know it, but they were walking directly toward Major Blake and his men.

Chapter 32

Above them, Hudson saw his son and Sarah's daughter heading for trouble. His plan to ambush the soldiers before they could spring their ambush on the Meat Co. guards was about to go sideways. If he shouted to get Rapscallion's attention, he would give away his position and likely draw the soldiers' fire.

However, doing nothing wasn't an option either.

Cursing his luck, he slipped out of his hiding place and started down the rocks. Rapscallion and Gabrielle had already passed him and he was going to have to run to catch up if he wanted to turn them around before they walked right into the Major Blake.

Jumping the last eight feet, he landed on both feet and tucked in to a roll to absorb the impact. Springing back to his feet, he ran through the gulley, heading for the trees.

He reached the first low-hanging branches, ducking around them as he chased after the kids. But when a cry of alarm from Gabrielle echoed through the leaves, he knew he was already too late.

Chapter 33

Rapscallion sensed the approaching soldiers before he saw them, but he wasn't fast enough to turn himself and Gabrielle around. In the space between heartbeats, he realised they had gone the wrong way and saw the first of Major Blake's elite soldiers emerge through the trees ahead.

They were caught in a small clearing, guns pointing their way as more of the black-clad soldiers came into sight. With their hands raised in surrender, Rapscallion questioned if the thieves would just shoot them.

No one fired though, giving Rapscallion a small amount of hope. His father was here somewhere, and he had been planning to ambush these guys. Was he about to charge through the bushes, gun blazing?

"What have we here," asked a deep voice. Striding through the midst of the soldiers, who had fanned out through the trees in every direction, the man with the steel-blue eyes and short cropped grey hair levelled his gaze at the two kids.

"You were at the time base," Major Blake said, addressing Rapscallion. "And now I find you here." He gave a small shrug and lifted his gun, an ugly black assault rifle. "Too bad for you."

Rapscallion gasped; Major Blake was going to shoot them.

Mercifully, Rapscallion's guess was wrong.

"Tie them and gag them," Major Blake commanded. "No sound. The rest of you, continue to the objective. We have wasted enough time here already."

Two of the soldiers came forward, releasing their weapons to let them hang by the slings as they took cable ties from their pockets.

It was a relief that they weren't going to be shot, but Rapscallion suspected it would prove to be a temporary reprieve.

"My dad is coming," he warned, working to keep his voice from trembling. "He's not someone you want to mess with."

Rapscallion's comments seemed to amuse Major Blake. "Little boy, I have a whole squad of soldiers, what can one man do against us?"

Rapscallion didn't get to answer. He didn't need to. Without the slightest warning, a shot came from behind his head and Major Blake's left shoulder erupted, an arc of blood spraying into the air from the bullet that hit him. He fell back, reeling from the wound.

More shots followed the first, Hudson careening through the trees as he took out three of the black clad soldiers before they could even begin to react.

Rapscallion felt like punching the air! His dad was coming to the rescue, just like he knew he would, but there were still so many of the soldiers to deal with and they were ready now. As he watched, they were all twisting to face the direction of the latest threat: his dad.

Horrified, Rapscallion couldn't see how they could escape now. Major Blake was hit, but in the half second since the bullet hit and he crashed backwards to the ground, he was already shouting orders and trying to get up.

"Rapscallion!" shouted Gabrielle, terrified for good reason and convinced there was about to be yet another gun battle, only this time with the two of them right in the middle of it.

Sensing the same danger, Rapscallion threw himself at Sarah's daughter, tackling her to the ground just as the soldiers opened fire.

Rapscallion heard his father shouting his name, calling for him through the cacophony of ear-splitting noise. He craned his neck, looking up from where he lay on the ground. His father was behind a tree, which gave him cover, but it was being peppered with bullets and wouldn't last.

Their situation was desperate, but a trumpeting roar even louder than the gunfire told him and everyone else it was about to get a whole lot worse.

The T-Rex pack was back!

Chapter 34

With so much background noise, no one had heard the giant carnivores approaching, so when they launched their attack, they were too close and coming too fast for the soldiers to escape.

Having rolled onto his back, lying against Gabrielle in the dirt, Rapscallion watched, his mouth open and his heart racing.

Two members of the T-Rex pack burst through the trees scooping soldiers as they came. A single bite was all they needed to end the frightened screams, but they didn't pause to devour their prey, they charged onward, never breaking stride in their search for the next victim.

To Rapscallion's right, Major Blake's men abandoned their quest to shoot his dad, swinging their aim to target the carnivores instead. That might have worked, and their first few bullets hit home, enraging the enormous beasts who flinched from the wounds stitching across their skin. But that was just two of the T-Rexes and Rapscallion's brain wasn't so terrified that he failed to question where the rest of the pack could be.

Three more entered the clearing from the right, coming from behind the soldiers. Like their comrades, their suffering was momentary.

The brighter of the soldiers understood the futility of trying to fight and chose to run away. Vanishing into the trees, they scattered in all directions.

"No!" roared Major Blake. "Stand and fight, you fools!" He was on his knees and getting up. The left sleeve of his jacket was soaked with blood from the wound Rapscallion's dad inflicted, but even though he grimaced against the pain, it didn't look to be slowing him down.

Unable to take his eyes away from the sight of the T-Rex pack tearing through the soldiers, Rapscallion had to feel to find Gabrielle's hand. Gripping it tightly, he knew they needed to get up. Running away wasn't a great strategy, but it was the only one he could come up with. Shooting the dinosaurs didn't work, it just annoyed them. His feet didn't want to move though, and it was only when the alpha looked their way that sheer terror sparked his legs to life.

His dad arrived just as Gabrielle and Rapscallion were scrambling to their feet. He was out of bullets, the small calibre handgun too feeble to do anything against a T-Rex anyway. It was tucked into a back pocket once more and all but forgotten.

Hudson grabbed both kids. Major Blake was five feet away and a serious threat still. If he chose to he could shoot them all. However, the Major's eyes were trained toward the T-Rex alpha and trying to wrestle his weapons away would only delay their departure.

The alpha roared again, voicing her rage at the humans. Caught in her glare, Hudson and the two kids stared back at the face of one of the world's most terrifying predators and knew what it must have felt like to be a herbivore in the Cretaceous – never able to truly feel safe knowing such terrible death could be hiding around the next corner.

The rest of the T-Rex pack had scattered, separating to pursue their own targets through the trees, but the alpha female didn't need the help of her pack to kill a few humans.

Pulling Rapscallion and Gabrielle back toward the trees, Hudson's only thoughts were about how to get away. They backed up a few feet, leaving Major Blake to face the T-Rex alpha alone and when he felt they were close enough to the trees, Hudson turned the kids around and started running.

The last thing Rapscallion saw, glancing back just before the press of trees stole his view, was Major Blake pulling out a large knife. His gun was discarded, out of bullets no doubt, and he was squaring off to face the one-armed T-Rex one to one.

A roar filled the air, but the scream Rapscallion expected to hear never came.

Running through the trees, Gabrielle held Hudson's left hand, Rapscallion held his right. They were all out of breath, mostly from fear and adrenaline, but also from the fifty yards they had just sprinted. He slowed, keeping hold of the kids' hands so they slowed too. Not because they were tiring or because they were out of breath, but so he could get his bearings. In all the confusion, he wasn't sure which way he had come and needed a moment to reorientate himself.

Since he last saw Sarah five minutes had ticked by and in that time a pack of T-Rexes chose to attack. Were the Meat Co. security team still pinned down? Had the soldiers back at the bogged vehicle scattered like their comrades in the ambush party?

People were still shooting, but it was sporadic now, not continuous like it had been when they arrived. Also, the bark of the .50 Cal mounted on the armoured vehicle had gone quiet and Hudson took that to be a good sign.

Checking the position of the sun where he could spot it through the canopy of leaves overhead, Hudson set off again with confident strides.

"It's this way," he said, doing his best to give reassurance. However, his confidence was fake, and the sound of something large approaching through the trees made them start running again.

Moments later, they broke through the trees at the edge of the forest. It meant they no longer had any cover to hide behind and if a T-Rex spotted them ... well, they all knew what that would mean.

So the sight of their battered dino rover bearing down on them at speed came with blessed relief.

"That's my mum!" cheered Gabrielle, relieved and elated to see her behind the wheel.

It wasn't just her mum though, Uncle Ralph was in the passenger seat and there were two more of the Meat Co. security guards in the back.

Sarah drove straight at them and cranked the wheel hard as she jammed on the brakes. The rover ploughed sideways through the loose dirt in a sideways skid, Sarah's worried face staring at them through the open driver's window.

"Get in!" she yelled.

They needed no such encouragement, Hudson helping Gabrielle and Rapscallion through the rear door before shouting for Sarah to go as he gripped the frame and launched himself inside.

The rover was moving before he could get his trailing foot off the ground, Sarah gunning the engine so it took off like a scalded cat. Hudson tumbled to the floor inside the rover, fighting conflicting forces of inertia and gravity. The door slammed shut, narrowly missing his toes when he pulled his legs inside.

Spikey, curious about the human on the floor by his face, tried to lick Hudson's cheek before Rapscallion scooped the baby dino onto his lap.

Uncle Ralph leaned through the gap, giving his brother a hand to right himself.

"Are you okay?" he demanded to know. "Are you hurt?"

"No," Hudson levered himself up and onto the back seat. "No, I'm fine. How about you?"

"I'll be fine," Uncle Ralph winced.

"He's been shot," revealed Sarah, spelling out what Uncle Ralph chose not to say. "It's not good. He needs a doctor."

"Others are hut worse," Uncle Ralph countered. "I'm not losing that much blood."

"Yes, but the medical supplies are all back at Time Base Alpha," Sarah pointed out. "If we don't get you help soon …" She didn't need to finish her sentence; everyone knew what it would mean if they couldn't get him back to their own time period. There he could receive proper medical treatment and his injury would be concerning but quite fixable. Here, in the Cretaceous, his wound was life threatening.

Hudson checked Gabrielle and Rapscallion, making sure they were okay before sliding between the front seats to check his brother.

Sarah, still driving, though not at the same breakneck speed she had been, twisted in her seat to find her daughter's eyes.

"You are grounded, young lady. You scared the life out of me. What were you thinking? Taking off like that?"

"Muuuum," Gabrielle whined.

"Don't you 'muuuum' me, miss. We have one rule. It's always been the same rule. Out here you do what I say. You don't ever wander off or go exploring. What if something had happened to you?"

"I was with Rapscallion," Gabrielle replied, her voice quiet because she knew there were no excuses her mother was going to accept.

"And what is he supposed to do when a T-Rex tries to eat you?" Sarah was close to hysterical and getting louder with each response.

Hudson, done with checking his brother, placed a hand on her shoulder.

"It's okay."

"It is not okay!" Sarah blurted, louder than ever. Then, more quietly, and with a tear running down her cheek, she added, "She's my only child. I cannot have anything happen to her."

Hudson nodded. "I know." He felt exactly the same about Rapscallion. He would give everything to protect his son. Even his life if that was what it took.

Silence descended, everyone keeping their own thoughts while Sarah followed the other surviving rovers back to the convoy.

Chapter 35

After the madness and high tension of the battle and subsequent T-Rex attack, the calmness of the drive to rejoin the convoy felt out of place.

Rapscallion's nerves kept him on edge. Choosing to follow his dad instead of getting in the rover with Sarah like he was supposed to almost cost his life. Worse yet, he put Gabrielle in danger and his dad too when he had to come to rescue them.

He needed to make better decisions and swore to himself that he would do so from now on.

Outside his window, the vast plains of the dinosaur world were filled with majestic beasts. He'd been watching them lazily for the last five minutes, but identifying and noting the different species: Nemegtosaurus, Nedoceratops, Panaplosaurus ... he realised he was looking at just as many species he couldn't identify.

"Sarah?"

"Yes?" She answered without turning her head.

"Who is naming the new species?"

This time she did turn her head and most of the rover's occupants paid attention to hear the exchange.

"You mean all the dinosaurs we can see here that no one has found fossils of?"

"Precisely," Rapscallion nodded. "Over there is one that looks like Saltasaurus, but it has a distinct brow ridge and it is bigger than the fossil records in my books."

Not for the first time, Sarah was impressed by the young boy's knowledge. She had always hoped Gabrielle would show the same interest she had in the strange prehistoric creatures, but while her daughter expressed some desire to learn palaeontology, the fervent, foaming-at-the-mouth craving for more knowledge was missing.

In contrast, Rapscallion had it by the bucket load.

"You have a good eye," Sarah remarked. "I have been compiling a list of the new species I have seen and have names for all of them. That one I call Browsaurus due to the same brow ridges you identified. However, the International Code of Zoological Nomenclature – that's the body who approve names for new species, are still arguing about how they can accept names for species no one else has ever seen."

Hudson frowned. "But surely you can take photographs to show them the new species you discover?"

"Ah, yes, I can and I have, but in the age of digital photography and artificially intelligent image creation, it is very easy to generate fake pictures. They want to be sure they avoid the trap of publishing information that later turns out to be false."

"So you need to bring other palaeontologists back here? Or people from the code of nomenclature?" Hudson tried to find a way around her quandary.

Sarah huffed out a slow breath – she had exhausted all these avenues already.

"There are three other palaeontologists here and we have submitted joint papers. I think they will be acknowledged in due course, but getting anyone else back to the Cretaceous comes down to Meat Co. and they are only interested in making money. Scientific bodies such as the Code of Nomenclature are not offering to pay for their passage, so Meat Co. denied them the opportunity to come here."

Rapscallion was listening, but his attention was split between what Sarah had to say about some boring old scientists and the far more interesting dinosaurs outside. Ever since their discovery, people had argued over dinosaur skin colour. Some fossils had been found with an impression of the skin intact, but were they grey? Brown? Tiger striped? Palaeontologists could only guess. Until now.

He was blown away by the range of colours on display.

"Meat Co. are planning to film documentaries," Sarah continued, "though they haven't given a date for that to start yet. They can see the profit to be made, and they have plans for a park with captive dinosaurs. It will be a bit like a zoo, I suppose, but they have to bring all the equipment and building materials through the time portal, so these are all concepts for now."

"How badly will the loss of Time Base Alpha impact them do you think?" asked Hudson.

"It will slow them down, for sure," Sarah conceded.

Groaning when he moved, Uncle Ralph had something to say.

"I think it will be worse than that. The government has been breathing down the firm's neck since the operation started. When they get wind of the reactor meltdown, it will give them all the ammunition they need to force Meat Co. to succumb to oversight restrictions. The government will pass laws to manage time travel and Meat Co., plus anyone else who ever enters the arena, will have to obey."

Hudson leaned forward to check on his brother. He was growing paler and though not in immediate danger, there was no denying his need for hospital treatment.

The conversation lulled, no one saying much until Gary, one of the security guards in the back said, "Hey, what's that?"

Chapter 36

For once it wasn't a dinosaur he was pointing at. Nor was it anything that was going to place them back in mortal danger.

Gary had spotted something that didn't belong.

With the forest behind them again, they were travelling across open plains which was how they were able to see something in the middle distance that defied explanation.

"It looks like a piece of machinery," frowned Hudson.

Sarah eased her foot off the accelerator pedal, allowing the dino rover to slow.

"Machinery?" she questioned. "What would that be doing all the way out here?"

Not only was it miles from Meat Co's primary operation, the random piece of equipment was enormous. Sarah couldn't think of one reason why it would be all the way out here. To her knowledge there had never been any operations in this area.

"Maybe it was abandoned years ago," suggested Gary.

Hudson shook his head. "No, you can see tyre tracks leading to it. Someone was here recently."

Sarah turned the wheel to the left, surprising everyone when she broke off from the back of the line of dino rovers. They were crammed with the surviving security guards and cutting across country to rendezvous with the main body of the convoy once more. Their destination was less than ten miles away now and getting there ought to be their only focus.

"Um, where are you going, Sarah?" asked Hudson. "We need to get to the convoy."

"I think this might be important," Sarah argued.

"More important than my brother's life?" Hudson was getting ready to wrestle the steering wheel from her if he needed to.

With a groan of pain when he shifted in his seat, Uncle Ralph offered his opinion. However, contrary to Hudson's expectation, he agreed with Sarah.

"I'm fine," lied Uncle Ralph. "Sarah might be right. This could be important."

"How?" Hudson did nothing to hide the exasperation in his voice. They were on their way to the original time base where they could realistically hope to escape the Cretaceous and return to their own time period. How could anything be more important than that? Especially given the state of his brother.

Shifting in his seat once more, as he fought to find a comfortable position, Uncle Ralph said, "There were some guys at the time base a few months ago. Real arrogant guys, you know. They upset a bunch of the guards."

"I remember them," said Gary. "There was a rumour that followed when they left."

Rapscallion and Gabrielle were absentmindedly petting Spikey, but their heads were tracking the conversation, twisting back and forth like they were watching a tennis match.

Hudson adjusted his expression, and unable to deny his own curiosity he asked, "What was the rumour?"

Uncle Ralph twisted around in his seat. Doing so hurt and he winced, but there was no denying the sparkle in his eye when he gave a single word answer.

"Gold."

Chapter 37

"Gold?"

Leonard Willis nodded his head just once. "Yes, gold. Among other things. Your task is to eliminate the people who are about to find out about it."

Standing before him in his private office high above Time Base UK, were members of Silent Solutions, a high-end security firm owned and run by one of Leonard's former school friends, Douglas Fotherington-Gill. Douglas wasn't present, but it was his old school chum to whom Leonard's first phone call had been placed.

Douglas had owed Leonard a favour for years and tonight was the right time to call it in.

The team leader, a man who introduced himself only as Barclay, wanted more information than he was being offered. His boss made it very clear the job was a premium rush and the bonus on offer for successful completion was greater than all the money he'd earned the previous year.

"That's the location outside Nottingham, yes?"

"That is correct."

"How much gold are we talking about?"

"Approximately four hundred tons. You don't need to worry about moving the gold itself, I have people on the ground to handle that already. However, it is about to be discovered and I cannot allow word of it to make it back here."

Leonard panned his eyes around the room, meeting the gaze of every man present. There was an even dozen of them including their leader, and Douglas assured him they were all highly capable individuals with no moral compass that would interfere with what he needed them to do.

"Time is of the essence, gentlemen," Leonard rose to his feet, "so let us not delay."

Barclay narrowed his eyes. "As I understand it, there are Meat Co. personnel trapped in the past. Are these the witnesses you wish to be eliminated?"

Leonard paused. Was this going to be a problem? He told Douglas to send him men who would kill on command. Now they were looking at him as if his requests were unreasonable.

Unsure where he now stood, Leonard opted for brutal honesty.

"Yes. Is that a problem? They are in my way and technically they have already been dead for sixty-five million years."

Barclay gave a slight dip of his head. "No problem at all, but I don't think the proposed bonus will cover it."

A smile quirked the edges of Leonard's mouth. He recognised this. He was short on time and his need was desperate, therefore they were in a position to negotiate. He was already offering them more money than he believed any would have ever seen before, but it didn't matter if he gave them even more.

"Shall we say double then?" he offered.

"How many of your staff are you expecting us to have to kill?"

"It's not just staff," Leonard admitted. "There was a tour taking place at the time of the accident. Assuming they have all survived, there were forty-two of them which brings the tally to something close to a hundred and fifty people. But, like I said, technically they have been dead for millions of years."

"But are there not also staff from the present on their way to the base in Nottingham to recommission what they believe to be a mothballed time portal? I take it you need us to eliminate them as well?"

"No, I will take care of them. They will be stopped at the gate."

"Won't that seem suspicious?"

"Deeply, but if you have an alternative plan, I am all ears."

Barclay knew it was time to play hardball. "I think we should call it treble what was originally offered. Killing innocent civilians can be taxing."

Muttering under his breath, Leonard grumbled, "Very well. Treble it is. Now, can you please get moving?"

Chapter 38

In the dino rover, Hudson was still trying to bend his brain around what he was hearing.

"Think about it," Uncle Ralph encouraged. "Back here no one owns the mineral rights. There are no countries, no borders, no rules. If you found a huge piece of diamond sticking out of the ground, does it belong to you?"

Sarah was horrified by her own naivety. It had never occurred to her that there might be people who would see time travel as an opportunity to exploit the planet's natural resources. That she worked for the same firm made her feel sick.

By mutual agreement, they had let the other dino rovers continue on their way to catch the convoy in favour of exploring the strange machine. As they drew closer, they got a better impression of its size.

It was stupidly big. Too big to have come through one of the time portals which meant it had been delivered in parts and built here.

Sarah stopped the rover just a few feet from it, leaving the engine running when she opened her door to get out.

Hudson opened the back door and climbed out too, closely followed by everyone but Uncle Ralph who knew he was better off staying put.

"Ever seen anything like this before?" Sarah asked.

She got head shakes in response.

Rapscallion placed Spikey on the ground, letting the baby dinosaur explore while the adults inspected the huge machine.

It towered over them, but it was a basic piece of engineering. Rock was fed into a hopper at the top where it fell through a grate into a crusher and along a series of conveyor belts. The exact workings were a mystery, but what it was used for proved easy to determine: there was gold dust everywhere.

All around them the ground had been dug over, the recent signs of excavation undeniable.

Hudson looked to the distance where they could still see the rovers from the battle kicking up a small dust cloud. The gold mining was interesting, but time remained his brother's enemy, and they needed to get moving again.

"We should go," he called to Sarah and the others. "We can report this when we get back, but getting left behind is a bad idea."

Their detour to inspect the machine hadn't taken them far from the route they were following, but Hudson was right; they needed to go. The convoy was ahead of them and might even be at the company's original time base already.

Back in the dino rover and moving again, Sarah said, "You see what this could mean, don't you?"

Hudson shrugged. "Someone is getting rich?"

"Super-rich. Money beyond the level most people can understand."

"Okay. So what?"

Sarah craned her neck around to look at Hudson. "It's all being done in secret, Hudson. Everyone thinks the time base we are heading for is out of use, but the gold they are mining must be going back to the present through it."

With a jolt of realisation Hudson saw what Sarah was trying to say. An operation like this one was worth billions or even trillions. If they were using the old time base to smuggle the gold out, they had sewn a web of lies to protect their secrets and given the amount of money involved, they had to be willing to kill to stop the world from knowing the truth.

The convoy with the staff from Time Base Alpha, plus all the tourists were heading for the original time base thinking it would be their salvation, but they could just as easily be about to walk into a trap.

Had the people back home figured out that Time Base Alpha had been compromised? Hudson guessed they must have, but what would that mean? Meat Co. were behind the gold mining operation. Meat Co. were the ones who chose to pretend the base in Nottingham was no longer in use. Would they even allow the refugees from Time Base Alpha to return through it? What were they going to find when they got there?

Chapter 39

Stacey Longbridge was half asleep when her driver stopped the car, the change in motion enough to jolt her awake.

"We are here?" she mumbled, hoping she hadn't been snoring.

"Sort of," the driver responded.

She was going to ask what that meant when she saw for herself. They were in a queue of cars lined up outside the gate to Time Base One – the Meat Co. premises just outside Nottingham. Peering through the windscreen to the line of cars ahead revealed nothing.

"What the devil is going on?" she demanded grumpily. It was drizzling outside and to get an answer Stacey could already see she was going to have to get out.

The driver had no answer for her, and though Stacey knew she could send him to find one, whatever he learned would then probably generate ten more questions. No, if she wanted answers Stacey was going to have to go herself.

"Is there an umbrella in the boot?" she asked, her tone hopeful.

Her driver looked up at his rearview mirror, meeting her eyes when he said, "I'm afraid not. Shall I see if anyone else has one?"

Stacey told him not to bother and didn't care that she made it sound like the rain, the time of day, and her lack of breakfast were all his fault. Slamming the door behind her, she stomped off through the rain to find someone she could shout at.

On the way to the front she passed six cars, two minibuses, and eight trucks. They contained about half the scientists working at Time Base UK and all the equipment they believed they would need to get the Nottingham time portal operational again. It hadn't been used in almost a year and while in theory it ought to turn on and work instantly, they wanted to be certain they had all the spare parts they might need.

They also had a portable decontamination unit loaded into one of the trucks. Stacey had no idea where it had come from, especially at such short notice, but there was a chance the Meat Co. personnel had been exposed to dangerous levels of radiation so the decontamination unit was a prudent precaution.

"What's going on?" asked Trevor Anglish, the firm's press officer, calling to Stacey through an inch of open window when she passed. She ignored him, pressing onward. If he wanted answers he could jolly well get out of his car like her.

Getting closer to the gate she could see people gathered ahead. Stacey could also hear their raised voices.

"You have to let us through!" The demand came from a man and though she couldn't see who had spoken, Stacey believed it was Max Armstrong. He was known for bullying his way through life, probably because the universe chose to stop him growing when he was five feet two inches tall. He compensated for his lack of height by employing his voice and through a generally unpleasant demeanour.

"Excuse me," Stacey politely forced her way through the gaggle of people to get to the front where Max was poking an angry finger into the chest of a security guard. The guard was more than a foot taller, and he was armed, but Max showed no sign that he cared.

"I swear it will cost you your job if you don't open these gates, young man," Max threatened. "There are people counting on us and I don't care what orders you might be following, the current situation supersedes them."

The guard had a colleague who was equally tall, equally broad, and looked equally unmovable. He looked down at the finger poking his chest and back up at the tiny man attached to it.

"No." It was a simple response. "The gates stay closed. Our orders are to deny anyone access and until such time as we hear different, that is how the situation will remain."

Max exploded, shouting and screaming at the guard until Stacey placed a hand on his shoulder.

Employing a soft tone, she said, "Thank you, Max. I will take it from here." She introduced herself as the firm's second in command and insisted the gates were to be opened.

However, the guard shook his head again, a bored expression on his face.

"That's not going to happen, Mrs Longbridge. Our orders are quite simple. No one gets in."

"And who gave you such an order?" she asked, wondering how long it would take to get the police here and whether they would be able to make the armed guards open the gate.

However, all her thoughts went sideways when the guard spoke again.

"Who told us to keep you and everyone else out? Leonard Willis."

The sound of a helicopter flying overhead drowned out what she said next, but seeing Leonard's private aircraft landing on the helipad was enough to change her thoughts anyway.

She took out her phone. Leonard was here. She hadn't expected that, but when he failed to answer and the doors to the helicopter opened to reveal what looked like soldiers getting out, her sense of confusion switched to one of utter bewilderment.

Chapter 40

Mercifully, catching up to the back of the convoy was easier than expected. Sarah had to drive fast to do it, but they were driving across flat plains again and were able to see the dust cloud the convoy created from a long way off.

The fleet of dino rovers carrying the staff from Time Base Alpha and the tourists from their abandoned dinosaur safari were moving in a gaggle rather than a straight column, and at a safe pace that made it possible for Sarah to go around the vehicles to get to the front.

They were looking for Robert Banks and Captain Cutter, the two men they needed to convince.

"There," Rapscallion shouted, pointing through the side window. "That's Captain Cutter. I can see his hair."

He was right, and it looked as though Robert Banks, the Meat Co. Senior Vice President was in the seat next to him.

Honking her horn madly, Sarah angled her wheels on a collision course with the lead vehicle. The faces inside registered shock, but she made sure to veer off long before they might think she was actually going to ram them.

Waving her arm out of the window, she shouted for them to stop.

"It's that stowaway again," Captain Cutter growled. "Keep going."

The driver gave a sharp nod and continued driving.

"They're not slowing down," Sarah remarked, almost unable to believe it.

"Then get in front of them," Hudson suggested. He wished he was driving, but any concerns he held about the palaeontologist being brave enough to do what was needed faded in a heartbeat when she gunned the dino rover's accelerator.

Glaring through her side window, Sarah shot the driver a look that threatened to melt the skin from his face and drove straight at him.

He yelped in fright and swerved out of her way. Fighting to keep his vehicle from flipping, he wrestled the wheel while behind him in the back seats, Robert Banks and Captain Cutter shouted their surprise.

"That's not quite what I had in mind," admitted Hudson, gripping the back of Sarah's driver's seat and holding on for dear life.

She grinned. "Worked though, didn't it?"

There was no denying that the convoy's lead vehicle was slowing down now.

Kicking his door open, Robert Banks yelled, "Are you crazy?"

The convoy was coming to a stop behind them, but the lead vehicles were already stationary and the people inside were getting out.

Sarah had likewise stopped her dino rover, parking it across the front of Robert's to be certain he wasn't going anywhere until he'd heard what she had to say.

"Hey, Sarah!" Robert yelled again. "What's wrong with you?"

She was out of her rover, but yet to pay him any attention. She was still talking to Hudson about how they were going to explain what they had seen and what they believed.

"Kids, I want you to stay here in the rover, okay?" she asked.

Captain Cutter, a replacement weapon he'd taken from another guard tucked into his holster, stormed after his boss, likewise intending to get answers.

Verbally disarming both men before they could say anything else, Sarah snapped, "What do you know about the gold mining?"

Robert's mouth stopped moving just as he was about to speak.

"Gold mining?" he repeated her words as though trying them on for size. "What are you talking about?"

Captain Cutter looked equally mystified, so either they were innocent, which met with Sarah's expectations, or they were world class actors. She took a few moments to describe the machine they found and explain about the recent tracks leading to it.

"This is utter garbage," spat Captain Cutter. "I've never heard such nonsense. No one is mining for gold in the Cretaceous era. The idea is utterly barmy."

Hudson asked, "How far are we from the time base now?"

Captain Cutter had been ignoring him, but shot him a warning look now.

"Is this your idea? What game are you playing now?"

"No game," Hudson met his gaze with emotionless eyes. "How far to the base?"

"Less than five miles," replied Robert when Captain Cutter failed to answer.

"Then in however long it takes us to cover the final five miles, you will see that we are right, or you will not." Hudson's calm delivery and reasoned approach was hard to fight.

Struggling to believe what he was hearing, Robert Banks asked Sarah, "You really think someone is using the old base to smuggle gold back to the present day?"

"I do. But like Hudson says, we will find out soon enough. The old base is supposed to be long abandoned and hasn't been used in months, right?"

"More than a year, I should say," Robert corrected her assessment.

With a grim tone, Hudson said, "Then we should expect it to be overgrown. I'm willing to bet it isn't."

Chapter 41

Robert Banks couldn't believe his eyes. His last visit to the original time base was more than a year ago and at that time construction at Time Base Alpha was finished so the old base was already out of use. To his knowledge, no one had been there since. They moved the operation more than one hundred miles south, closer to the firm's headquarters which was a sensible move for a number of reasons, but none of drivers to move south had ever been expressed as a need to secretly dig up the world's supply of gold. And that was what it looked like they had done.

Reading the land, Hudson had guided the lead vehicles to a bluff a quarter of a mile from the base. Looking down onto it from higher ground, the size of the mining operation was staggering.

There were no people in sight at all, though there was evidence of recent activity in the form of tyre tracks crisscrossing the area. A few trucks and other vehicles were parked to one side, but not enough to account for the huge piles of gold bars stacked in the open for all to see.

Rapscallion didn't know how much gold was stored in Fort Knox, the home of the US gold reserve, but he was willing to bet it wasn't as much as he could see right now.

"Is it safe, Dad?" he asked. Spikey the triceratops was tucked under his arm.

Upon hearing the question, Robert Banks turned his head to look at Rapscallion's father. He'd told them the old base was still in use and had been right about it. Also, according to the security guards he sent to retrieve the time vortex generator, his intervention saved their lives. If there was a person present the Meat Co. Senior VP was going to listen to, it was Hudson Gilbert.

Seeing that everyone waited for his opinion, Hudson flipped a mental coin. They couldn't see anyone below and that probably meant the old time base was minimally manned. The gold mining operation wasn't taking place here – they had to go to where the gold could be found. So the miners were elsewhere, but there remained a risk that the people behind the gold mining had figured out the Time Base Alpha refugees would head there and discover what they were doing.

So, the old time base might look unmanned but could be hiding dozens of armed men waiting to ambush them.

Ultimately, they had to find out one way or another. The time portal was their only way home.

Taking a deep breath, Hudson said, "I'm going to go down there. I want three guards with weapons. We are going to take a fast drive through the area to see if there are any nasty surprises waiting for us."

Captain Cutter volunteered to be one of the men to accompany Hudson, and there were plenty of others who raised their hands.

Rapscallion didn't like it, he only had one dad and this sounded dangerous.

"It's necessary, Rap," Hudson was on one knee, his head level with his son's. "But it's just a precaution. I don't think there is anyone there."

"You can stay with me and Gabrielle," Sarah offered, putting an arm around his shoulders.

The guards mounted one of the dino rovers, opening the windows so they could aim their guns outward in case they needed to shoot.

They were ready to go, but Hudson made them wait a little longer.

"Son, you need to leave the baby dinosaur here." He said the words with compassion, making them sound like an apology, but he also had to be firm. Taking the triceratops home was never a tenable proposition.

Rapscallion hugged Spikey a little tighter. "But he's so little, Dad. We can't just leave him here. Anything could happen to him. Can't we just help him to grow a little bigger and then bring him back?"

"No, son. I'm sorry, but he needs to stay here."

Hudson hated that Rapscallion was upset. He really needed to get him a pet of his own. Maybe this wouldn't be so bad if he had a dog at home to get back to.

Sarah tried to help, by saying, "There are some triceratopses over by those trees." She pointed. Half a kilometre away, a small herd of the horned behemoths were grazing in the open at the edge of a forest.

"Mr Gilbert," Robert Banks called. "I'm afraid time is against us." He held his electronic tablet in the air. "The reactor core cannot last much longer."

Hudson really didn't need anyone to light a fire under his butt to get him moving. His brother's condition was enough motivation if the simple need to get his son home wasn't. Thankfully, there were qualified medics amongst the staff from Time Base Alpha, so Uncle Ralph was at least getting some treatment.

"Sorry, Rap," he cupped his son's chin, making him look up into his eyes.

"I know, Dad. You've got to go. Just ... be careful, okay?"

They hugged, Rapscallion letting Spikey go for a moment to put both arms around his father.

"Mr Gilbert," Robert reminded gently.

Breaking the hug, Hudson saw his son had tears in his eyes, but whether they were born of fear for his father's safety or the need to send the baby triceratops back to his own kind, he could only guess.

Pushing himself upright, he got into the driver's seat of the dino rover, checked the guards were ready, and got it moving. When he glanced in his rear-view mirror, Rapscallion was with Sarah and Gabrielle, all three heading for their battered dino rover. Hudson hoped the baby triceratops would play along and be happy to see its own species. It would be so much harder if it tried to cling to Rapscallion.

Pushing such thoughts from his mind, he concentrated on the task at hand. He drove in a winding route that took him around the bluff and past a small copse of trees to get to the old time base. A pack of hadrosaurs drinking at a pond lifted their heads, honking to each other as the strange thing drove by.

Approaching the mining trucks and piles of gold, no one inside the dino rover spoke. Their eyes were in constant motion, aimed this way and that in their search for anyone who might be trying to hide.

The central building was far smaller than Hudson had expected. Unlike Time Base Alpha, which boasted gargantuan proportions, the old time base was no more than the size of a small industrial unit – about twice the size of a modest house. Brick built, with a large roller door on one side, it looked like nothing much at all until one noticed the enormous generator and the cables running from it to the building. There were two barnlike structures to the west and a row of portaloos backed against one side.

Hudson drove at a steady pace – neither fast nor slow, and was ready to accelerate at the first sign of an ambush. It was quiet though. There was no one around as though the base was completely abandoned.

WE ARE NOT MEAT

Aiming for the very obvious front entrance to the time base beneath a big sign boasting 'Meat Co.', Hudson pulled to a stop. He let the engine idle, everyone in the dino rover remaining silent and watchful until he finally spoke.

"I guess we can call the others forward then. It looks like the place is safe to use."

He was about to add how relieved he was to be wrong when the front doors flew open.

Chapter 42

With two sets of guards to accompany them, Sarah drove their dented, scarred dino rover as close to the triceratops herd as she dared. She didn't want to spook them by going too close, but equally didn't want to have to walk too far carrying Rapscallion's baby dinosaur.

Whether the pack would accept Spikey she genuinely didn't know. There were examples in the world of nature where female animals would adopt an infant, but whether the same could be applied to dinosaurs was something they were about to find out.

Rapscallion placed the baby dino at his feet, angling its body so he could see the giant herbivores.

"Will these guys do?" he asked, crouching to be next to Spikey's head. "Can they be your new family? They look nice." Truthfully, Rapscallion didn't know if they looked nice at all. They were giant things though there were some smaller ones among the pack he took to be juveniles. In all he counted nineteen of them.

Spikey was yet to show any interest.

"Perhaps we need to get him closer?" Gabrielle suggested. "Maybe they are too far away for him to see."

"We don't want to get too close," warned Sarah. "They might charge if they feel threatened."

Rapscallion witnessed a dinosaur stampede first hand just the previous day and had no desire to relive it. He needed to do something though because he refused to leave Spikey in the open by himself. Only if he joined a new herd would Rapscallion believe his little friend would be safe.

"Come on, boy," he called, encouraging Spikey to follow as he started forward.

Sarah opened her mouth intending to warn him not to go much farther, but a sound caught her ears, and she held off speaking while she tried to figure out what it was.

Rapscallion edged closer to the herd. Spikey was keeping up, but making no attempt to leave his human companion behind and the giant triceratops ahead were making Rapscallion nervous. They were watching him intently and in the space between the next two heartbeats, one turned to face his way.

It dipped his head in a display that reminded Rapscallion of a bull getting ready to charge. It was enough to stop his feet moving.

Twisting at the waist, he looked behind to where Sarah and Gabrielle waited by the rover. Behind them the guard escort waited in their vehicles, paying little attention to what he was doing.

Rapscallion said, "Um." He wanted to ask Sarah what to do, but she wasn't looking his way. At least, not exactly. She was looking over his head to the trees beyond the triceratops. There was a sound coming from them, a low buzzing, droning sound.

It was familiar. Rapscallion knew what it was, but before his brain could supply the name for it, Sarah started shouting.

"Rapscallion!"

The urgency in her voice sent a jolt of fear through his body.

"Get back here! Fast!" Sarah was beckoning with one hand and ripping open the dino rover's door with the other. Bundling Gabrielle inside, she shouted that he should run before jumping into the driver's seat.

Confused and a little scared, Rapscallion twitched with indecision. He knew he needed to run – this was the kind of place where you run when someone tells you to – but he was supposed to be reuniting Spikey with his own kind. So should he leave the baby triceratops to join the herd by himself, or should he grab him so they could try again later?

The buzzing, droning sound was getting louder and it was accompanied now by the sound of tree branches being swatted aside. Then a thumping sound filled the air and Rapscallion knew precisely what the new noise was: the triceratops herd were charging.

Eyes wide and mouth open, Rapscallion stared at the oncoming danger, but only for long enough to see what had got them moving. Crashing through the forest behind them was the armoured vehicle.

There were bits of tree sticking out of it at random angles where branches had snapped off but been snagged, and there were members of Major Blake's team of thieves visible in the front windows, their black uniforms easy to pick out even at a distance.

Behind them, the trees continued to shake and sway because the armoured vehicle was being pursued. By the pack of T-Rexes Rapscallion discovered when one charged through the trees and into sight.

Rapscallion was already running by that point, a trifecta of dangers hot on his heels. Ultimately, it wouldn't matter if he got crushed by a triceratops, run over or shot by major Blake's thieves, or eaten by a T-Rex. Death was death whichever way it came, but carrying Spikey in his arms and pumping his legs for all he was worth, he hoped to stay alive at least a little while longer.

Sarah jabbed on the brake, stopping the rover right in front of Rapscallion. Out of breath he threw himself through the back door almost before Gabrielle got it open.

Sarah screamed, "Hold on to something!" and took off again. The guard escort that came with them was way ahead, leaving Sarah and the kids behind to save themselves. They were halfway back to the convoy and honking their horns to alert everyone to the imminent danger heading their way.

Her teeth gritted hard together Sarah prayed someone had activated the time portal. They were heading for it at speed and nothing or no one was going to stop her going straight through it.

There had been no sound of gunshots, so she could only assume Hudson's concern for an ambush had proven unfounded.

Chapter 43

Outside the time base Hudson's right foot hovered over the accelerator pedal, ready to catapult them away from danger when the doors flew open and a figure emerged.

Captain Cutter, hanging out of the passenger side window, aimed his gun squarely at the chest of the first man to exit the building and pulled his trigger.

The sound of the shot echoing inside the dino rover hurt Hudson's ears, but didn't deafen him so much that he couldn't hear himself shouting, "Nooooo!"

The bullet hit the framework next to the door, missing the target by more than a foot.

Mercifully, Captain Cutter only fired the one shot before realising the person he was shooting at was just an unarmed Meat Co. worker.

"Good thing you're a terrible shot," Hudson remarked snarkily, shoving his door open to get out.

The Meat Co. worker, a man wearing overalls and work boots had darted back into the building and could now be heard shouting to whoever was inside with him.

With a sigh, Hudson jumped out of the rover and started for the doors.

"Come on!" he shouted when no one followed him. "He probably thinks we are here to steal the gold. Let's explain things before he arms himself, shall we?"

Captain Cutter and the guards ran after Hudson, catching up as he went through the door.

"Helloooo?" Hudson called out, making his voice sound friendly and unthreatening. "Helloooo. Sorry about the twitchy trigger finger. We are not here to steal the gold."

There was no one in sight and apart from the steady hum of the generator outside, there was no noise. The building's interior was nothing like Time Base Alpha. There were no pens filled with dinosaurs, there were no dino rovers parked in neat lines, and there were no giant open spaces.

It was all one room, with a series of offices against the far wall. Banks of monitors and huge cables ran from the offices to a smaller version of the same black liquid screen Hudson recognised at the time portal. This one was still operational, he noted with a sigh of relief. All they had to do was activate it and they could all go home.

"This is Captain Cutter from Time Base Alpha," Captain Cutter called out loudly. "Please show yourselves." He waited, listening for a reply that didn't come. "Time Base Alpha has suffered a massive reactor leak. I have more than one hundred Meat Co. personnel and tourists with me. They need to use the portal to get home."

Still no response came back, but the sound of a door banging open was followed almost immediately by the sound of a vehicle starting. Its engine roared as whoever was inside it chose to be somewhere else.

Hudson ran back outside and around the corner of the time base to see a truck barrelling across the Cretaceous plains to get away.

Turning around to find Captain Cutter and the guards looking at him, he asked, "Anyone know how to operate the time portal?"

They didn't, but Captain Cutter promised there were others in the convoy who did. They were about to go fetch everyone when the sound of honking horns and panicked shouts filled the air.

One of the guards muttered, "What now?"

Hudson didn't know what might have befallen the main body of the convoy, but before they could react, they spotted all the dino rovers heading their way. They were all aimed at the time base, but unlike the orderly procession of vehicles that made their way north from Time Base Alpha, this looked to be a case of every person for themselves.

They were driving too fast and all coming at once, racing each other to get to the time base first.

It was hard to be sure, but Hudson couldn't spot 'his' dino rover. The rest of the fleet, apart from a little dirt and dust, were still pristine. His rover looked like it had been through a war. Where was Rapscallion? Where were Sarah and Gabrielle?

The first vehicles to arrive screeched to a halt, the occupants leaping out and running.

Captain Cutter shouted, "What's going on!" as they raced past him.

His question was answered by Robert Banks, the Senior Vice President arriving in the very next rover.

"T-Rex pack!" he blurted. "Charging triceratops!" Running up the steps toward the time base doors he grabbed Captain Cutter's arm and dragged him through. With the door swinging shut, he added, "And those murderous thieves are on their way too!"

Hudson ran up the steps so the added height would give him a better view. Dino rovers were pouring in from every angle, the people in them parking to the left and right. Men and women, security guards and scientists alike were all racing to get away from the menace chasing them and there was still no sign of his son.

He spotted Angus huffing as he shifted his bulky frame as fast as it could go. Then he saw the medics helping the wounded, which included Uncle Ralph. It made them slower, so Hudson ran to help, assisting those less able to get into the old time base.

Handing off the man he'd helped and making sure his brother was okay, Hudson ran back outside to look for Rapscallion again. He was starting to feel desperate and the procession of dino rovers was thinning, the final few coming now with no sign of 'his' rover anywhere.

Cursing that he had let Rapscallion out of his sight, he ducked his head through the door to check on progress inside. The offices at the far end were full of people, the banks of monitors now displaying reams of scrolling numbers.

They were activating the time portal and not a moment too soon.

The last two of the dino rovers skidded to a stop, guards hurrying from both sides.

"Where's my kid!" yelled Hudson, determined to stop the guards and get answers if he needed to.

"Still coming!" shouted one, aiming an arm back the way they had come before running around Hudson to get inside.

He wasn't lying. A hundred yards behind everyone else, the battered and almost broken dino rover careened into sight. It swept around the trees and into the open and was moving so fast it looked to be barely under control.

The inner wheels all but lifting off the ground as it shot across the Cretaceous dirt.

Hudson ran back down the steps, going to them even as they were racing to get to him. He couldn't see Rapscallion, but had to believe he was in the dino rover with Sarah and Gabrielle.

He had to be.

The noise from the generator doubled in volume, the surge and the cheer that followed it making Hudson believe they must have opened the time portal. It was almost over. All he had to do was get Rapscallion out of the dino rover and through the portal. They might face criminal charges for trespass when they got home, but he didn't care about that right now. So long as he got Rapscallion home and safe, nothing else mattered.

His breath caught in his throat when the herd of adult triceratops broke through the trees. Some of them had gone around, but moving about as fast as they could go, the huge armour-headed beasts covered too wide of an area and some went straight through the trees like they were twigs.

Robert said the T-Rex pack was back and though Hudson hadn't doubted it, a bellowing roar from one of the mighty carnivores drove home how close they were.

Cheering and shouting from inside the time base filled Hudson with fresh hope. Sarah would hit her brakes in the next two seconds and all they had to do was get inside. They were far enough ahead of the charging triceratops that they could almost walk and still make it safely through the portal.

They didn't do that though.

The moment Sarah's vehicle came to a stop, Hudson wrenched open the back door.

"Rapscallion!" he cried with relief.

Sarah and Gabrielle jumped out just as Hudson pulled his son's arm.

"Wait, Dad. Spikey is still with us. He didn't get the chance to join the herd."

Startled to find the baby triceratops still in the dino rover, Hudson knew there was no time for a discussion. He scooped Spikey under one arm, grabbed Rapscallion's hand with the other, and ran.

Sarah and her daughter were just ahead, on the steps and heading for the doors.

Hudson shouted, "Go!"

The triceratops herd was bearing down on them at speed. Maybe they would go around the time base and keep going, but Hudson had seen what they did to the trees. They were being chased by a pack of carnivores and the abandoned dino rovers were creating a funnel. Once they were between them, it seemed inevitable that they would run into the front façade of the time base. They would damage it, possibly even bring it down, and Hudson planned to be through the portal before that could happen.

Darting through the doors, he was shocked to find there was no one there.

"They've all gone through already!" said Sarah.

Tugging his father forward, Rapscallion yelled, "The portal is still open, Dad! Let's go!"

Conscious that he was still carrying a baby triceratops, Hudson ran through the old time base. The time portal was in the middle of the building, the flat, black screen of liquid facing them. It was mounted a few feet off the ground on a raised platform just like it had been when they went through the first time. Could that really have been less than two days ago? It felt like they had been in the Cretaceous for weeks.

Unlike the cautious approach they took the first time, nervously stepping up to the black liquid and pausing before going through, this time they charged at it, running full speed until they plunged through and felt their bodies elongate once more.

The strange sensation made Rapscallion feel a mile thick again, but with a snap the light returned to his eyes and he tumbled through and out of the other side.

Where he found himself faced with a dozen armed men holding machine guns.

Chapter 44

Outside the base gates Stacey Longbridge was surprised to see Timothy Moore when he arrived.

"Tim? What are you doing here?"

"I've come to ruin Leonard's plans. He's mining gold, you know?"

Stacey blinked. "He's doing what?"

Twisting to look back the way he had come past the logjam of vehicles outside the gates, he raised a hand and waved for someone to come his way.

"I was approached by a branch of the government some time ago. I've been spying for them ever since and working with the police to figure out what he has been up to."

Stacey shook her head as though she could clear it with the motion. Still reeling from Tim's revelation about the gold, his claim to be a spy was making her head hurt.

Coming along behind him wasn't just one person, but a whole squad of them. They were police in tactical black uniforms and each of them was armed to the teeth.

"Good Lord," she blushed. "You're not kidding about the gold?"

"I'm afraid not. I was trying to gather evidence, but if you are right about the Time Base Alpha staff making their way north to get home via the original portal, then I am greatly concerned Leonard plans to kill them all."

"What!" Stacey couldn't believe what she was hearing.

"He's mining for gold in the past, Stacey. There's no law against it which is why the police haven't moved against him yet, but he cannot be allowed to bring it back to our time. It will cause untold havoc and destabilise the global economic market."

The police had gone around them and were now arguing with the same pair of security guards behind the Time Base One gates. Just as before, they were refusing to let anyone through.

Chapter 45

To their left, the Meat Co. employees and the tourists were on their knees. They had their hands on their heads and a small pile of the security guards' handguns showed they had been disarmed.

Captain Cutter sported a bloody lip where he must have resisted.

"Anyone to follow?" asked Barclay. "Are you the last ones?"

Scared and confused about what was happening, Gabrielle said, "Mum?"

Hudson had no such confusion. He'd predicted an ambush. The only part he was wrong about was the location. He expected them to attack in the past, but they chose instead to wait for the weary refugees to make it back to their own time period. Now they could kill them and dump the bodies back in the Cretaceous. No one would ever know, and their bodies would never be found.

WE ARE NOT MEAT

"Are you the last ones?" Barclay repeated his question, raising his voice so it was almost a shout.

Hudson gripped Rapscallion's hand a little tighter, counting in his head and praying he was right. They had left the time portal open, so anything that touched it would be brought through from the past to the present.

Grinning to convey he knew something the men with the guns did not, Hudson said, "Not exactly."

A piece of broken brick landed by his feet. It had come through the portal.

His cryptic reply and the surprising piece of rubble caused a moment of confusion in which Hudson chose to move. Yanking Rapscallion with him, he ran across the front of the time portal. Shunting into Sarah and Gabrielle, he took them with him, launching himself and everyone else out of the way just before the first triceratops emerged at speed from the inky blackness of the time portal.

Barclay had enough time to draw a panicked breath before the tip of the nose horn smashed through his rib cage. The men to his left and right were slammed out of the way by the dinosaur's unforgiving frill. Designed to protect it from giant Cretaceous carnivores, a puny human stood no chance at all.

The triceratops didn't stop or even slow down when it mowed through the line of armed men and not one of them got a shot off. When a second animal followed the first a half second later, the line of men found themselves scattered and trying to stay alive.

Captain Cutter jumped to his feet, shouting to rally his force of security guards, but a volley of bullets stopped them before they could close the distance and overwhelm Leonard Willis's assassins.

The pair of triceratopses had trampled five of the armed men before running through the wall to make a new exit, but seven remained and they were the only ones in the building with guns.

Noting Barclay's broken body, his second in command, Allan Shepherd, took command, firing over the heads of the frightened civilians.

"I think it's time to end this," he remarked, his voice devoid of emotion. "Take aim."

A cacophony of panicked cries and terrified wails filed the air as the armed men swung their guns around to point at the huddled mass of people.

Two more aimed at Hudson, Rapscallion, and the girls. There was nothing they could do, no time in which to react.

However, when the first shot rang out, it was Allan Shepherd who fell. Coming through the portal were the ragged final members of Major Blake's team of tech thieves. Led by a battered and bleeding Sergeant Hawk, they were still armed and hellbent on escape. It was not for the sake of the Time Base Alpha refugees that they shot the assassins, but their simple desire to escape what was behind them. The men with the guns stood in their way and that spelled their doom.

The assassins fired back, and seeing the opportunity to regain control, Captain Cutter lunged for the pile of handguns. More of his guards went with him, arming themselves and joining the firefight to aid the refugees' escape.

Certain they wouldn't get a better chance, Hudson yelled, "Everybody run!" With Rapscallion at his side, he leapt to his feet, drove a punch at one of Major Blakes thieves, and barrelled through his falling body.

With a glance to check Sarah and Gabrielle were still with him, he ran for the doors. He had no thought to look back, the building was utter bedlam with three different factions of people fighting, but when a T-Rex bellowed, he couldn't help but turn to see the mighty beast coming through the time portal.

Just like the triceratops, whether by accident because it was going too fast, or deliberately when it chose to follow the humans, it was in their time period now and trapped in a room with a mountain of yummy targets.

Chapter 46

With no one to bar their way, the bulk of the Meat Co. personnel were running for the doors. Or straight out through the hole the triceratops made.

Hudson, Rapscallion, Sarah, Gabrielle, and even Spikey the baby dino, were among them. The air outside was fresh, sweet, and filled with the scent of fresh rain. The grass beneath their feet was damp, but they noticed very little of that.

A roar from the T-Rex filled the air, the enormous volume of it making the very bones inside the humans quiver.

Barclay's team of assassins, those who were still alive, had scattered. Major Blake's thieves hadn't so much as paused when they came through the time portal. They had been getting chased by the pack of T-Rexes for hours. Their one remaining armoured vehicle was significantly slower than the dino rovers and barely able to keep ahead of the pack. Running at full speed, a T-Rex was faster and they had only just made it to the second time base before they ran out of fuel.

Landing back in their own time period, they had no thoughts other than to escape. Finding armed men blocking their way, they did what came naturally: they opened fire.

The police hadn't argued with the guards at the gates for long. The sound of panicked screams coming from the other side, closely followed by people shooting was all the justification they needed to force the gates open.

They ran into the compound only to stop dead in their tracks when a pair of triceratopses jogged by. Before they could get moving again, and questioning which of the buildings ahead was the one they wanted, people started to appear.

They were running for all they were worth. Some in suits, some in security guard uniforms, others in ordinary clothes. Yet more were dressed as soldiers, all in black and they appeared to be armed. Reacting to the sight of guns, the head of the police armed response unit, Chief Inspector Hector Daniels, barked a command.

He changed the command a heartbeat later when the end of the building to his front exploded outward in a shower of brickwork and a one-armed T-Rex emerged.

Nothing in his training or his career to date had prepared him for such a moment, but though almost crippled by fear, he ordered his officers to open fire.

WE ARE NOT MEAT

The tyrannosaur was an easy target to hit, but their bullets didn't cut it down the way the police expected. When the first few struck home, gouging the dinosaur's skin and leaving pockmarked wounds on its chest and flank, it turned tail. It ducked back inside the building to get away, and when silence fell, the police cautiously moved in.

Along the way they dealt with anyone else who appeared to be armed, arriving nervously at the ruined wall through which they saw the T-Rex vanish. Aiming their weapons into the dust-filled interior, they expected to find their target and were ready to open fire, but of the T-Rex there was no sign.

"Where did it go?" asked one of Hector's officers.

He had no answer, but the giant rectangle of inky black liquid gave a hint.

They switched the time portal off a few moments later, the police fetching one of Stacey's technicians to operate it once they were confident the area was safe.

Hudson and Rapscallion watched from the other side of the compound. They had found a low wall to sit on. Just across from them, the pair of triceratopses, a male and a female according to Sarah, had found some bushes on which to nibble. Between them and looking quite content, Spikey ate his fill too.

Chapter 47

No one knew about the private time portal located in a nondescript building on the far side of Time Base UK's lot. Leonard had it installed 'just in case' when the contractors were building everything else.

Unaware of the events unfolding at the Meat Co. building in Nottingham, he believed the potential drama was managed. The private security team would eliminate any witnesses attempting to get back through the original time portal so it wouldn't matter that they had seen his gold mining operation. He could fire Stacey Longbridge and the rest of the employees who had gone to Nottingham. Oh, there would be questions to answer, and the government were going to find out about the reactor meltdown and subsequent radiation leak, but he had teams of lawyers to handle them.

Confident he would be able to hide from whatever political fallout came his way, probably on his private island in the Caribbean, Leonard donned his radiation suit. It was the best that money could buy and came with a guarantee to protect the wearer for periods of up to one hour.

He only needed five minutes.

Just like at Time Base UK, he had a private office in Time Base Alpha. There, he had a giant chunk of diamond. It was one of the first diamonds his mining teams found and was bigger than anything ever recorded in modern times.

He didn't need it, he was rich enough, but he planned to have it polished and mounted in the entranceway to his London house in Mayfair. It would set the right tone for anyone who came to visit.

Activating the portal, Leonard stepped in and through, arriving a second later sixty-five million years in the past. He exited the building in which his secret time portal at this end was located. Much like the one at Time Base UK, it was housed in a nondescript building for which he held the only key.

Inside his radiation suit, he began to whistle, content everything was going his way. Just like always.

He strolled through the empty time base, a little saddened to see such a bright beacon of his empire now sitting unused. Taking the stairs, he made his way to the second floor and used his keycard to open the door to his office.

The huge hunk of diamond was hidden inside a cupboard on the far wall. But Leonard didn't get to retrieve it. The reactor, which had been near tipping point for almost two days, chose that moment to overload. It exploded with a force roughly equivalent to six Hiroshima bombs going off at once.

Leonard and Time Base Alpha were vapourised in an instant, the nuclear explosion scattering Cretaceous wildlife for more than a hundred miles in every direction.

A hundred miles north of Leonard and Time Base Alpha, the workers who ran away when the refugees arrived were returning. They had help with them in the form of a dozen miners, but they proved to not be needed.

There was no one there, but staring in shock at the utterly ruined building in which their time portal still appeared to be intact, they were looking the right way to see the mushroom cloud when it filled the distant sky.

Epilogue

In the aftermath that followed the news of Time Base Alpha's reactor meltdown, the scandal about Meat Co's gold mining operation, and the unexplained disappearance of the firm's owner, no one thought to charge Hudson with trespass. He'd broken a bunch of rules sneaking into Meat Co's UK base to take Rapscallion on a dinosaur adventure, but the people at Meat Co. were hailing him a hero.

The survivors who fled Time Base Alpha claimed he was one of the chief reasons they survived and acted as though they believe he tricked the triceratops into coming through the time portal to defeat the assassins Leonard hired to hide his secrets.

Uncle Ralph was rushed to hospital along with almost half of the survivors, many of whom were injured in the final moments of their ordeal when the T-Rex appeared. He was going to be fine though. An operation to remove the bullet followed by several weeks of rest would do the trick.

Rapscallion was looking forward to seeing his uncle again, but for now was quite content to watch Spikey trotting around his new pen.

The time portals were not broken, and even if they had been, it would be possible to build another, but the British government, backed by politicians from around the world, had stepped in to shut down all time travel.

At least until they could control it and put laws in place that would ensure there could be no more rogue operations such as Meat Co's.

With a universal ban on opening the time portals, the three triceratopses were stuck in the present, but that wasn't proving to be much of a problem. They had been moved to London Zoo where tourists were queuing for days to get a look.

Rapscallion didn't have to queue though. More than willing to take the dinosaurs, London Zoo needed a keeper and there didn't appear to be anyone who knew anything about their diet or behaviours. Until they discovered there just so happened to be a Swedish palaeontologist with the three triceratopses when they went to collect them. She had arranged with the zoo for Rapscallion to come and go as he pleased.

WE ARE NOT MEAT

Sarah said she wasn't planning to stay in London long term, but Rapscallion had a sneaking suspicion his dad and Gabrielle's mum liked each other.

Dangling another whole lettuce, he waited for Spikey to wander over to the bars to take it from his hands. Reaching through, he stroked the side of the baby dino's frill and grinned when it burped at him.

His ninth birthday had come and gone, the gifts, cake, and cards fading in his memory. He wasn't going to forget his trip to the Cretaceous though. Not ever.

The End

Author's Note:

Hello, Dear Reader,

This book came as a complete departure to everything I have written to date and features a genre it was never my plan to broach. It came about when Hunter, my eight-year-old son, and I took a trip to the Natural History Museum in London. They run overnight events called Dinosnores and Hunter is about as dinosaur mad as any other kid on the planet.

We spent the evening exploring the dinosaur exhibits by torchlight, sitting in child friendly lectures given by real palaeontologists, and taking part in other dinosaur related activities. Settling down to sleep beneath the tail bones of Sophie, the world's most complete stegosaur skeleton, he came up with the concept for this story.

I helped him flesh it out and together we threw ideas around until we had something that had to be labelled a 'time travel dinosaur adventure'.

WE ARE NOT MEAT

We started writing it the very next day. And I mean 'we'. Hunter physically wrote about ten percent of the book, slowly tapping out the words with two fingers and constantly asking me how to spell words.

Obviously, the more complicated elements came from my brain, but the desire to include a baby dinosaur was all his. He wanted a palaeontologist in the story who would be running dinosaur safaris and he insisted on the T-Rex pack to act as a constant danger throughout the story.

The central bad guy, Leonard Willis, is mining for gold and other precious minerals in England. You may not associate Britain with gold, but plenty of it has been found here. Just like everywhere else, precious gemstones and deposits of rare metals sit below the ground just waiting to be found. I wanted the money-mad billionaire to be up to something nefarious and loved the idea that he would abuse time travel to steal the gold millions of years before anyone else could get to it.

The plan is to write at least two more books, returning to the central figures you have already met. They will find themselves thrust back into the drama in each instalment and Hunter and I have a fun idea for how it will all end.

My son is resolute in his desire to be a palaeontologist and likely has the brain to pull it off. He may very well choose a different career as he grows, but I hope he continues to write no matter what he does.

Take care.

Steve Higgs

Free Books and More

Want to see what else I have written? Go to my website.

https://stevehiggsbooks.com/

Or sign up to my newsletter where you will get sneak peeks, exclusive giveaways, behind the scenes content, and more. Plus, you'll be notified of Fan Pricing events when they occur and get exclusive offers from other authors because all UF writers are automatically friends.

Click the link or copy it carefully into your web browser.

https://stevehiggsbooks.com/newsletter/

Prefer social media? Join my thriving Facebook community.

Want to join the inner circle where you can keep up to date with everything? This is a free group on Facebook where you can hang out with likeminded individuals and enjoy discussing my books. There is cake too (but only if you bring it).

https://www.facebook.com/groups/1151907108277718

Printed in Great Britain
by Amazon